Pia the Pinena Fairy

Saving Maui

Written & Illustrated by

Amy Zhao

This is a fiction story.
Names and places in this book are the product of the author's imagination or used fictitiously. It is pure coincidental if they resemble any actual thing.

I feel blessed to be able to finish writing this book, and there are so many people I want to express my thanks to.

To Sunrise Elementary, Northshore School District.

> I love the wonderful learning experiences in the classroom, in the library, and on the campus. I want to say thanks to all the great teachers, students, and all my friends.

To all nearby communities.

> Kenmore, Bothell, Lake Forest Park, Redmond, Kirkland, and greater Seattle. While writing this book, as well as for my previous books, I met with many delightful local young readers. As I talked with them, in their eyes I could clearly see their desire and passion for reading, writing, and exploring. That gave me the warmth and energy to keep writing. I also got many encouragements from their parents. Thank you.

And so many others... Thank you!

Table of Contents

Prologue 1

Chapter 1
Slate of Chaos 3

Chapter 2
The Friendship Clue 21

Chapter 3
Lending a Tail 35

Chapter 4
The Ocean's Blue Wonder 46

Chapter 5
Commander Crusher's Mission 54

Chapter 6
The Darkest Doom 56

Chapter 7
Captured by Pirates! 66

Chapter 8

    The Secret of Friendship 82

Chapter 9

    Commander Crusher's Secret 90

Chapter 10

    A Close Call 94

Chapter 11

    The Cursed Key 99

Chapter 12

    The Fairy of Darkness 114

Chapter 13

    The One Shows the Way 140

Chapter 14

    The Fall of the Coral 149

Chapter 15

    Whom to Sacrifice? 160

Chapter 16

    The Challenge 168

Chapter 17

    Sour Snakes 176

Chapter 18

    The Center of the Maze 193

Chapter 19

    Death of a Friend 210

Chapter 20

    The Friendship Point 236

Chapter 21

    The Last Attempt 265

Chapter 22

    The Final Battle 274

Chapter 23

    Saving Friendship 293

Pia the Pinena Fairy

PROLOGUE

Hi! I'm Pia the Pinena Fairy. Pinena means traveler in fairy language. I love to travel and I have great adventures. Along the way I meet and make new friends. Yes, my talent is Friendship.

In my previous adventures, I have unlocked the epic, mythical Moondust Mine. With which I reversed the fate for cursed Magicores, so they became friendly and cheerful again. Along with that, I encouraged my bird friend Harmonica to build friendship with her old archenemy and together, they won The Best Bird of the Year contest.

In another adventure, I traveled with my friends through the forest of monsters and had many close encounters. We scaled the Magic Mountains and had to battle a fire-breathing dragon before we received valuable and trusted advice from The Legendary Judges of Magic and saved the day.

In this story, I need to travel to the beautiful Maui, Hawaii. But I'm not going there for vacation. I'm on a mission with my friends, the Friendship fairies of Maui. My friends are in grave danger. Maui's fate is resting in our young hands. But all this is nothing compared to the rumor about the master plan from the darkest villain of the world, Slate of Chaos.

If the mission fails, this might be the last time you hear from me...

Wish me luck.

Read on to join me in this daring adventure!

Chapter 1

SLATE OF CHAOS

"Where is it?" a voice demanded. "Tell me, where is it? And the fairies?"

"I'm sorry, they escaped, sir." A giant dark black spider whimpered. "We can look for the stone, though!"

The drapes hung like shadows in the dark, cold room. A vase sat at the corner of the room, its shadow encasing the contents. Small spiders scuttled at the corners of the room, avoiding the chair.

"We um, we will look for them any chance we get. The darkness can soon be restored. I promise, sire. I'm really sorry!"

"YOU let them ESCAPE!" bellowed the one in the chair.

"You let them ESCAPE! WHY? I don't remember that being part of the plan. Or did you improvise?" The chair creaked ominously.

"Lord of Chaos, please, you must understand." whispered the giant spider, tears streaking down his scarred face.

He stuttered nervously, desperately searching for words. "We do know that they are looking for the Friendship stones."

"You fool!" Slate of Chaos, the one in the chair screeched. "That is exactly what you should be doing! I have sent spies out to track the Friendship Fairies so they will have no progress. I have made the perfect plan. I will destroy Friendship!"

Slate hissed, and the spider could feel his fiery aura.

"Yet I have a FOOL as a commander!" Slate growled. "How, I say, how? I will not let this happen! Spin me." A gloved finger pointed at the corner of the room.

A giant spider crawled over, placed a skinny, hairy leg onto the chair's handle, and spun the chair slowly around. Then the spider quickly crawled backwards, kneeling down until his jaws rested upon the ground.

The chair Slate was resting upon spun around.

It revealed a magical being, a fairy with no wings.

Slate of Chaos wore a night-black suit that blended in with the shadows on the walls.

A heavy, gold chest piece rested on his shoulders, and what distinguished him from his black chair were pearl white gloves, complete with his white boots.

Placed in his hand was a shard of broken wing. The wing had blood stained on the edges, as if it had been freshly torn from a dying fairy.

Slate wore a deadly expression, and in his eyes could be seen a blade of fire, so strong, it would tear, destroy, eliminate anything in its path.

He flung the shard of wing away with an expression disgust and loathing.

"Fairies… Chair spider! You're dismissed."

The spider who had spun the chair whispered a hoarse thanks, then dashed out of the room without further hesitation.

The commander, who was the bowing spider, looked longing after the chair spider and burst into tears, his whole entire body shaking.

"Please, don't! Give me another chance! Please, my lord, Slate of Chaos. They are not easy to take from! I swear, I will succeed this time! I need time! I need better warriors!"

Slate sighed sarcastically, licking bloody lips. He turned his head away from the commander.

"Friendship. My archenemy, and a worshipped talent. How I hate it!" he blinked slowly, his gloved hand turning to a fist. "But they know it's not going to last. Their peacefulness is through."

"Please, sir. Please! I'll do anything! Anything!" the commander spider rolled on the ground. "I beg of you! You have already punished my father, mother, my brothers, and sisters, and all my other relatives, my uncles, aunts, and cousins! Please don't punish my family more!"

The door creaked in reply and the windows shattered in the chilly room.

A gust of wind brushed the leg hairs of the spider, who shivered in the icy stare of Slate.

"Oh, I won't harm your family this time. Just you." Slate looked coldly at him. "For you have failed me. I shall give you a place in the Whirling waters. You will not enjoy it. After all, it is a torture chamber, hm?"

"NOO!" Cried the spider. "Anything! Please don't make me go there!"

"Too late," Slate whispered softly. "your time is past."

The spider grimaced and more tears rolled down his face as if he knew what was going to happen next.

And as he did, two buff spiders swung the door open, filling the room with dim light, and dragged the wailing old commander out.

"I regret it." Slate smiled, showing uneven teeth. Though no remorse welled in his heart as he watched his old commander being dragged away.

The door slammed shut and darkness flooded the room.

Satisfied, Slate looked at his gloved hands and revolved them slowly. A red orb appeared, glowing in the dark and damp room.

The orb hovered in the air, offering dim light.

Slate watched it with a crooked grin plastered on his face as it gave the dark room an eerily glow.

"So, the Friendship fairies are moving again in search of their precious little stone." Slate muttered to himself.

"I shall find another commander and defeat Friendship once and for all! How glorious it feels, success. And beating the thing that once hurt me, and cut a deep scar into my soul."

He bit his lip a notch too hard. Blood came pouring out. Slate licked up the blood.

"I cannot stand it, and once I might have had friends. That was once. Friends are nasty, I can't even believe they even have such thing as a Friendship talent! I don't understand it at all. Ha…."

Bam!

Slate looked up as another giant spider walked in, thrusting open the door.

He was bigger than the last, and his jaws were clamped together menacing.

The spider walked forward steadily, and his stride was long and sturdy. Muscles poked out from his burly chest, and the hair on his legs tingled with anticipation as he nervously met Slate's gaze.

"State your business."

Slate whispered, eyes narrowed into slits.

"My name is Crusher, and I want to be your new commander." Growled Crusher, kneading the ground with a leg.

Slate raised an eyebrow.

"All your old commanders are pipsqueaks, too soft and fragile. I am stronger and cleverer than the rest of the spiders, mind you, the world probably." Crusher continued. "I am the only one worthy of leading your great army."

"Oh really?" Slate scoffed, toying with a strand of dark magic. "What gives you the idea? How will I know you will not fail me, like so many before you?"

He didn't let the great spider answer.

Clump.

Clump.

Slate walked across the room, circling Crusher. His boots showed no mercy to the ground as it cracked beneath his feet.

"You all know what happens if you fail to take the Friendship stones from the fairies." Slate hissed dangerously.

"The fairies have already escaped me twice!" Slate raged, holding up two fingers.

"I need to capture and destroy the two Friendship stones they hold, and the third once found!"

Slate paced back and forth. Crusher watched him silently. Crack. The floor was full of dents shaped like one's foot.

"I can help." Crusher offered again, puffing up his chest in confidence.

Slate stopped and rose up into the air on a thundercloud, glaring at Crusher through yellow eyes.

"You offer to help me. You offer to be a commander? Foolish!"

He whisked his hand into the air, and dark blue wind gusted from the shattered windows.

CREAK!

The door to his right slid open, to reveal many spiders being flushed down a whirlpool. Their screeches and yells echoed off the dark blue walls.

Plump - actually, FAT - Goblin sharks swam in the bloody water. They gnawed on long spindly legs and tore at flesh and bone. The whirlpool turned scarlet with blood, and the screeching never ceased.

Crusher gasped. His legs trembled, and he seemed to shrink in size.

Slate smiled.

"Don't worry, Crusher. The Whirling waters whirlpool has quite a nice power." Slate stared at Crusher through yellow eyes. "They who stay in it will live for eternity and feel the wrath of Slate of Chaos!"

Slate gave Crusher a crooked grin. "Most would rather be executed rather than stay in that wonderful torture chamber."

"Mwa ha ha ha!" Slate cackled, tilting his head back.

He clutched at his stomach, letting out another shriek of evil laughter. "Mwa ha ha h-"

"Excuse me, my Lord?" a bulking spider clutched at a checkboard. It shivered as Slate glanced at him. "May I have a moment?"

"HOW DARE YOU INTERRUPT MY EVIL LAUGH?"

Slate bellowed. "Especially when I was in the MIDDLE of it!"

"So sorry, sir, my apologies. Um, sir, I just…. We, the spies have located where the Friendship fairies are going next." Stuttered the bulking spider, bowing until his head touched the ground.

"And also, we found out that another fairy is aiding the three Friendship fairies. Her name is Pia the Pinena fairy. I think 'Pinena' means traveler in fairy."

"Well, oh!" Slate exclaimed, showcasing a delighted face. "Now there are four fairies! I can get rid of the fairies easily. More fun! More deaths! Hooray!"

"But, sir!" stammered the spider, biting his clipboard. "The Pia Pinena fairy, she is an expert at finding stuff, we've researched into all her past accomplishments, she found many things even the famous fairy so-called heroes could not find. We spiders fear, with her in the way, we will encounter more difficulties."

"Oh?"

"If I am commander I can destroy them!" Crusher burst out, jumping up and down.

"Crusher, shut up." Slate turned back to the spider. "Any more information?"

The spider nodded, then stopped. "Er, not really... sort of." He stuttered.

"Talk."

"The rest of the troops wonder of your true master plan. You have not shared it with us yet."

"They will remain in the dark then!" Slate ranted. "If they really want to find out my secret, master, grand, evil plan, they will use their brains! Of course, sometimes I doubt they have brains until I feel them in my very fingers! Why don't they add my hints together? It's as simple as adding one and one! Oh, wait. They can't do math, neither can they count. Pity!"

The spider just nodded.

"Also, taking what you said previously into account, I shall send out troops to ambush the fairies when the time is right." Slate spat on the ground. "How do you say her name?"

"Pia." Gulped the spider. "Pia the Pinena fairy, sir." The spider nodded again. Nodding seemed like the only useful thing he could do.

"Pia...The Pinena fairy must be stopped, if she is helping the Friendship fairies. Oh, and to remind myself, you still interrupted my evil laugh!" Slate grumbled unhappily.

"My apologies, sir, please forgive me! Oh, merciful Lord of Chaos, please forgive my actions! I wasn't thinking straight!" The spider whispered, rolling on the ground. "I'm useful, you might need me! Please! I'm your MOST faithful servant!"

"I don't show mercy, not even to my most trusted - and dead - commanders! TO THE WHIRLING WATERS!" screeched Slate, his eyes popping crazily. His arm waved once more.

With that, the spider was whisked into the water, the stunned expression still on his face. His clipboard clattered onto the ground.

Suddenly, a goblin shark leaped out of the water and toppled onto the spider.

"AAARGH!"

Slate turned towards Crusher, a casual look on his face as if he did this every day.

Only, he MUST have done that every day.

Blood rose in an arc into the air, and as Slate picked up the clipboard, the stream of blood pooled onto it, the perfect image of a certain dead spider.

Slate snickered, all his worry evaporating. "Doodles. I call this art!"

"I think I can get the Friendship stones." muttered Crusher, his eyes fixed on the Whirling waters. He looked around nervously at the rows of spiders guarding the Whirling waters.

"You think?" Slate questioned, his voice turned dark. "You must KNOW it!"

"I know!" Crusher glared at him, a foot scuffing the ground. "I want the big prize."

He backed up into the other room and Slate followed, slamming the poor door shut.

"Very well." Slate motioned to the ground in front of him. His yellow eyes had turned an evil shade of purple.

They glowed with mischief in the dim light. "Stand back."

Crusher leaped back into the wall with a loud crash, but Slate did not seem to care or notice.

Crusher toppled onto the ground. Behind him was a fairly clear shape of a large, bulky spider who had just crashed into the wall.

"Once from the dark, never to the light.
I summon you now with much delight.

Contribute your warriors to my commander,
But make them quick, make them fast,
So that the fairies will not last!"

Slate chanted, and a moaning noise started.

Suddenly, a swirl of dark magic leaped from the dark room and circled around them.

"What's happening?" Crusher growled, looking a bit scared for once.

Crusher had a notepad out and had jotted the curse down in gibberish, noting down every movement Slate made.

However, the words burned through the pad and Crusher dropped it, yelping in surprise as a small black flame issued onto his leg.

Crusher quickly blew it out, then looked at Slate, who was yawning sleepily. Slate's eyes were yellow again.

"These are just your new army of dark magic spiders. They are agile and flexible, able to do anything." Slate yawned.

Slate poked Crusher's hairy leg. "Hairy, oh my! Bet you never shave. How intimidating! A hairy spider is about to help ME defeat the Friendship fairies!"

Crusher protested, but Slate shushed him with a wave of an arm.

"Oh, the fairies will laugh themselves to death before you have the chance to lay one claw on them."

"You idiot! I trained my leg hairs! They can pick up movement and help me locate nearby targets! And you? You have no skills and rely too much on magic!"

Crusher hissed, then covered his mouth as he realized what he had just said to his boss.

"Pardon me?" Slate leaned forward.

His eyes dangerously glinted and he surveyed Crusher like a snake would before it finished off a mouse. "I'm rather sorry, didn't catch that."

"Nothing, O great Slate of Chaos." Crusher trembled, pressing his face to the ground. "Nothing, sire. Nothing you need to worry about."

Slate glared at him.

"Watch your big mouth, you wimp of an excuse of a spider! I let you off the hook this time."

The magic encircling them whirled around for a moment, then they formed into agile spiders of the spider army.

"Take your spiders and bring me the Friendship stones, Commander Crusher!" Slate ordered. "NOW!" He flicked his finger and the door to their side opened. "And get rid of all four fairies! Especially Pia the Pinena fairy!"

Crusher hesitated.

"Go!" Slate screamed.

Without another word, he disappeared into the darkness, leaving Commander Crusher and his new army of spiders standing utterly speechless.

Chapter 2
THE FRIENDSHIP CLUE

I could see it now.

I flew through the sky, flapping my rosy wings urgently. Wind whooshed through my ears and buffeted my hair.

The wide expanse of Maui's blue ocean swirled below me. The waves lapped at the shore of a golden beach, my destination.

I'm Pia the Pinena Fairy, just in case you were wondering.

It was warm in Maui but I didn't have time to enjoy the weather. I was to meet my friends on this beach. They must be expecting me! Oh dear, I hoped I wasn't late.

I looked up, seeing the dormant volcano Haleakalā looming over the beach.

Looking around with the bearing sun shining down on me, I checked my belt to make sure I had everything I needed.

My brown belt was covered with secret pockets that held many things. For some strange reason, my dad had insisted I never go anywhere without the pocket knife he had entrusted me with. My mom had made me a knife case in my belt.

My pocket knife would be actually useful if the blade part was longer, but at least it's a great accessory!

My lavender purple shirt billowed in the breeze, and I could feel the cool breath of the wind on my sleeves as my pink flower lei tingled on my neck.

Receiving a lei is a blessing. I was jumping with excitement when I got my lei. I crossed my fingers in hope my mission in Maui would be blessed and successful.

There was a flash of white as my pearl heart necklace reflected the beams of sunlight. My dainty red boots touched the sand as I landed on the sunny beach.

There was a yell and my three friends Faith, Olivia, and Lily dashed over wearing anxious expressions.

I waved back and flew closer to them.

I came here for a mission.

My old friend Faith contacted me. She needed my help urgently.

Faith was a Friendship fairy of Maui.

She and her two Friendship fairy friends Olivia and Lily share a big responsibility. They recharge Friendship for Maui - and the world. They do this by using their Friendship stones every ten years when Friendship starts to wither.

However, in order to recharge Friendship, it has to be done on a particular day before sunset.

And that particular day?

Today!

That's why my friends and I were so rushed.

But to make things worse, there's a big problem in our way - the evil villain Slate of Chaos.

No one knew the exact details about Slate and his power.

But legend says that Slate used to be a fairy man.

On a dreadful day, he lost his wings. Lurking in the darkness, Slate found out that by creating and feeding on chaos, his magical powers became stronger.

The fairies around him said that every day Slate was growing distant from them, darkened and harsh. Until finally one day Slate received extremely strong magic from mysterious figures.

The dark magic took control over him.

And Slate became the feared, powerful, Slate of Chaos.

Slate had only one weakness, which was our advantage - Friendship.

Determined to rule Maui with evil, Slate set out a plan to destroy the three Friendship stones, so the Friendship fairies can't recharge Friendship.

If Slate destroyed Friendship, he could create panic and trouble without Friendship in his way, feeding on the chaos like a bloodthirsty monster lamprey.

If we couldn't stop Slate now, he will grow stronger and stronger, and he would finally be able to take over Maui.

Maui and all the good creatures living here would DROWN in the darkness and evil.

I shivered and felt a light hand on my shoulder.

"Hey." Faith greeted me. "Good to see you again, Pia."

"You too." I suppressed a small smile. We hugged and Faith made some introductions. I nodded and shook hands with Olivia and Lily.

"Where is everyone?" I asked Faith, glancing around. "This beach strikes me as the type of hot spot that everyone would go to every day! I mean, look at the beach sand! It's so soft and the perfect spot to have picnics and stuff!"

"Everyone believes Slate of Chaos will win." Faith sighed dejectedly. "They've fought many battles against Slate, but they all failed miserably. Everyone in the battle perished, and Slate sought out their families and… murdered them, threatening to do that every time they battle him."

I gasped.

"Right now they're all in their homes, spending their time with loved ones before, they say, Slate..." Faith couldn't say any more.

"Oh, no!" I cried. "We better get going. Can I see your clue?" I bit my lip nervously. "You haven't lost it, have you?"

The Friendship fairies received clues to help them find their Friendship stones.

Olivia and Lily had already found theirs, leaving Faith the only one without her stone yet.

"I have my clue right here. Oh, Pia, I'm the only one without my Friendship stone! I feel so helpless, I haven't found mine yet…" Faith wailed. She pulled out a small piece of parchment from her Wing-on.

A Wing-on is a magical pocket which you attach to your wings. When you need it, it appears, when you don't need it, it disappears, an extremely useful item.

"My clue's smudged, and I can't make out what's written in the smudged part. Do you think you can help?"

"I'll try my best to decode it." I glanced at the parchment and sighed, racking my brain.

"ARR!" echoes through the dark cave,
The one ____ ____ shows the way,
_____ ___he snake of lies and mystery,
Cross the path of the twisted _____,
Retrieve your stone oh so true.

Olivia wailed. "Nothing in the clue makes sense!" She pointed at the parchment. "Look, the clue says 'ARR', which must be pirates. They live on high seas, but at the same time it mentions a snake, which is found on land."

"Associating pirates with 'ARR' is a good thing. And look at the next few words. 'ARR!' echoes through the dark cave…. maybe pirates are hiding in a dark cave." I suggested.

"Maybe we go into the ocean and then follow the clue onto land." Faith thought out loud. "But that doesn't make sense. Unless each sentence of the clue is linked to the other…"

I glanced at the clue, my open hand bunching into a fist in frustration.

"Maybe the one shows the way is a sign or a post of some sort," Lily suggested, then buried her head in her arms for a second. "No, that can't be right."

"He snake of lies and mystery……" I muttered. "Okay, given what we think so far, let's suppose that the Friendship stone is somewhere underwater. The 'snake' could be a sea snake, then."

"But what if the Friendship stone is on land?" Olivia countered, scratching her head. "Snakes are on land, just because the clue mentioned a snake doesn't mean it is a sea snake. And Faith is right.

28

Choose land or sea. The Friendship stone is hidden on land or in the sea."

"The clue also mentions pirates." I pointed out. "Pirates loot stuff, and on land they're called robbers or bandits. Pirates live on the sea."

"What could the clue mean?" Faith wondered, then shook her head. "Calm down, Faith. Calm down!"

"Snake…." Muttered Lily, tapping her chin. "How many snakes are there in Maui?"

"A ton." Olivia groaned, pinching her cheeks in frustration. "And out of a million creatures, which one is going to show us the way?"

"Stop!" Faith caught Olivia's hand. "Please don't beat yourself up, Olivia!"

I narrowed my eyes. If only the clue wasn't smudged!

Faith was quietly thinking. "We know that in the clue, 'cross the path of the twisted' part could be twisted kelp, vines, basically anything, anywhere!"

I nodded vigorously in agreement. "And in the clue, 'the one shows the way' could be anywhere, too. Or in other words, there are many varieties, like a librarian to show you where the history section is in a library. Or a map! Both those lines are very broad."

"We need to narrow down the possibilities. The clue is too vague." I read the clue once again. "Based on this, I think we should head for the ocean."

"I agree." Olivia nodded gravely.

"Me too. I want to save Friendship badly, and I'm willing to take a risk." Lily glanced at Faith. "What do you think, Faith? You get to decide where to go. It's your stone after all."

Faith squirmed in her position, deep in thought. "You want to go to the ocean, right, Pia? Do you believe it is the place my Friendship stone is hidden?"

"Positive." I nodded. "Today is the last day, we must remember to be smart but quick. I think we should head to the darkest cave in the ocean."

Faith blinked slowly, sucking in her cheeks. "Ocean and dark cave it is. But how are we going to get underwater? It's hard. First, the air bubbles we are able to produce are fragile, and secondly, they are not suited for long-term diving."

Fairies could produce two types of bubbles - an air bubble and a water bubble.

Air bubbles were commonly used for Diving talent fairies to help them breathe underwater. Meanwhile, the water bubbles were used as defense in battles.

I sighed, then thought of something.

"My mermaid friend Marissa should be able to help us. I know she's around here in Maui, and she could be an awesome guide to the underwater world." I flapped my wings, eager to get started.

Faith frowned, tension peaking. "But how do we get to Marissa, if we are heading to the ocean? The ocean is so big, to find one mermaid is hard! Not to mention to find my Friendship stone."

31

"Oh! I have a Wina, I'll contact her!" Lily piped up. "Does she have a Wina?"

"Yes, something similar," I confirmed. "Except that mermaids call theirs differently."

Lily pulled a Wina out of her Wing-on.

A Wina was home of a pixie that served its fairy owner. Lily had decorated her Wina with sapphires and rhinestones and added purple glitter to the pink surface.

Glossy rare portalan panes covered the Wina. Portalan was a special portal that connected Winas. Wings jutted from the Wina's sides, giving it a realistic glow.

"Buttercup! Can you help me with something?"

Lily shook the Wina slightly and a pixie came tumbling out from the glossy Portalan surface on the Wina.

"Good morning, Miss Lily!" Buttercup the pixie exclaimed, and straightened up, flapping her tiny wings excitedly.

She flew in a small loop-de-loop, her grassy hula skirt swaying in the air.

"What can Buttercup do for you today?"

"I need you to contact a mermaid in the ocean," Lily explained in a rush to Buttercup. "Can you do that?"

"Of course, Buttercup can!" Buttercup trilled eagerly.

Lily held out a jug of nectar to Buttercup and Buttercup took it gladly, chugging it down. She stopped with a burp, her pixie hat lopsided on her brown-red hair. "Buttercup do right away, now who does Lily need to contact?"

I informed her and Buttercup took off into her Wina in a rush. Olivia bit her nail but stopped when I noticed. Lily was watching the Wina intently.

"Pia?" Faith had edged to my side.

Her expression was glazed with fear and anxiety as she lowered her voice so that only I could hear.

"What if Marissa can't help us? What if I can't find my Friendship stone? What will happen then?"

I hugged her tightly, not knowing what to say. But a stick was lodged in my throat. What if Marissa couldn't help us? And what if we couldn't find Faith's Friendship stone?

Friendship - and Maui was resting on the shoulders of my brave mermaid friend.

Chapter 3
LENDING A TAIL

"Oh!" I gasped. A gale of wind hit me squarely in the face.

Buttercup the pixie disappeared into her Wina, and popped her head back out. She pointed at a spot in the ocean where a tall rock jutted out from the water.

"Do we meet this Marissa mermaid there?" Olivia asked, her red hair splayed on her face.

"Buttercup says 'Yup'!" Buttercup nodded, gurgling down more nectar relentlessly.

"Let's hope she can help us, then." Faith murmured, gazing at the water intently. "We don't have any time to waste."

I squeezed her hand.

The five of us (including Buttercup!) were flying over the ocean to meet my friend Marissa for help.

If we were heading towards the darkest cave in the ocean, Marissa would be a great guide. She might also be able to help us find a way to overcome the problem of our fragile fairy air bubbles.

Buttercup darted into the Wina and popped out. "Buttercup thinks a few more seconds, ack!" Her nectar jug slipped from her tiny fingers.

I darted forward to catch the jug at the same time as Lily. Our heads smashed together. The nectar jug slipped from our fingers and sank from sight.

I looked at the water and shivered as a gust of wind blew past my ears.

"Oh no! That was Buttercup's favorite flavor of nectar!" Buttercup cried, dismayed.

"Aw, it's okay, Buttercup." Lily comforted her, rubbing her head. "I'll get more." Lily broke off. "After we save Friendship."

No sooner had she said that, two mermaids broke through the surface of the water.

It was Marissa and her sister Emily!

Marissa held out the jug of nectar Buttercup had dropped and she smiled as Buttercup took it gratefully.

Marissa had brown hair with brilliant hot pink on the tips, and her tail was beautiful as ever. She wore a light kelp shirt supposedly made by the famous mermaid fashionista Elisa Tails, and shining bracelets hung from her right wrist.

Emily was Marissa's little sister. Her brown hair was braided, and her tail was pale pink with add-on make up glitter.

We made introductions and told Marissa about the Friendship stones and the clues.

Marissa nodded gravely, her emerald green tail flicking. "I have heard. You must be careful, you know Slate is following you. To help you with your mission, I discovered a flower in Maui that enables you to breathe underwater.

"It is called 'Ka hanu o ka moana', which means 'The Breath of the Sea'. I will get it, then I will lead you to the darkest cave in the ocean. Be sure of your decision."

"We have to get in those caves!" Faith nodded solemnly. "For Friendship!"

"Are you sure?" Marissa asked, then looked at me, uncertainty and worry clouding her gaze. "It's dangerous, anything can happen. You have to be sure before you decide to enter the cave. All of you."

"For Friendship."

I declared confidently with my other friends, but I couldn't help gulp.

Marissa met my eyes for a moment and I hesitated. "We're sure."

"Alright."

"THANK YOU!" Faith darted forward. "You don't know how much this means to me."

I thanked Marissa while Buttercup dizzied herself flying around.

"Anytime. Just lending a tail! Emily, stay here." Marissa gave a quick smile, then dove into the water.

Emily grinned. I pinched her cheek affectionately and she squealed, splashing me with water.

She didn't seem to understand the situation Maui was in. Instead, she was gladly taking the chance to show-off. "Look, Pia! Look what I can do!"

And as the surrounding fairies watched, Emily thrust her arms up.

Instantly a glob of water sprouted from the ocean like a fountain in a heart shape. Water spewed from the sides and a jet of water zipped overhead, creating an arc.

"Like it?" Emily smiled earnestly at me. "I've been working a long time on it. I finally know how to make a Water heart fountain level 2!"

"Awesome!" I exclaimed. "Emily, you've improved since I last saw you!"

My friends congratulated Emily, and she swished her pink tail from side to side happily, stirring up some water. "Gee, thanks! It was hard, but for now, that's all I can do!"

"Have you tried making a water bubble?" I asked Emily.

She shook her head. "I never tried."

"Here." I showed Emily how to make a water bubble.

Emily lifted her hands slowly, and a bubble of water formed and rose from the ocean.

It broke apart as Emily rapidly lost control.

"Wow!" Emily exclaimed, looking awestruck. "I held it there for nearly five whole seconds!"

"Awesome! You're a natural!" I smiled at her. "Try again, and use more energy to hold the bubble together. And after that, with more practice and good aim, you'll be able to shoot the bubble far away."

I demonstrated by cupping my hands together, forming a water bubble, and I hurled it far off into the distance.

Emily's brow furrowed as she raised her hands once more. This time she held it for a longer period of time before the water rushed into the ocean.

Marissa had surfaced behind me. She was just in time to see the end of Emily's practice. Her sides were heaving, but a grin was plastered on her face.

Her fists were clenched as she pulled up a flower. "I have the Breath of the Sea. And Emily, that was great! Keep practicing!"

Marissa pealed the petals of the flower, placing a petal into each of our outstretched palms.

The petals were bright green, and lines of pale yellow bordered the middle of each petal. Marissa trod water.

"This is the Breath of the Sea flower. You need to each take a petal of the flower and eat it." Marissa explained. "I think this should last you till about sunset. Better hurry and eat up, they only work when very fresh."

Emily reached out to grab the remaining petals. "Yum!" Emily sighed.

"This is good. Even better than Sea Star sorbet!"

"Will it have any side effects on Emily?" Faith wondered, finishing her share. "She already can breathe underwater."

Marissa shook her head. "It might give Emily a craving for more, but it should be fine."

We munched on the Breath of the Sea's petals quickly.

Buttercup gobbled down her share greedily and exclaimed, "Yum! Just like nectar! Buttercup wants to find more!"

"We don't have much time to spare." Lily gently told her pixie.

Buttercup drooped sadly, showing little tiny googly pixie eyes. "You can have some nectar on the way down in the water," Lily said kindly, pulling out another large nectar jug from her Wing-on. Buttercup flew in circles happily.

"Now jump into the water!" Marissa grinned, attempting to put a smile on everyone's faces. "Last one in is a grouchy lionfish!"

"But Lionfish aren't grouchy! Buttercup meet one once!" Buttercup protested, but her voice was drowned out by our loud splashes.

I leaped into the water.

SPLASH!

The impact of my jump sent ripples through the surface of the water.

I opened my eyes cautiously and glanced around, then timidly breathed in some water.

My eyes widened. My cheeks bulged.

Marissa's tail flicked, and the next second, she was in the water facing me.

"Breath, Pia! Come on, it's okay." Marissa encouraged.

I spit out air and sucked in the water. No liquid invaded my lungs or choked me.

"Fluttering Fairies! Wow!" I gurgled.

My friends were attempting to swim beside me.

Buttercup was hovering over the water. "Come on!" Lily pulled her in.

Emily was teaching the others the fastest way to move around, looking pleased she knew something the older fairies didn't.

My wings folded down by my sides, wrapping around my pink skirt like a protective cover.

I felt like a seal, twisting and turning in the water perfectly.

The others noticed my idea and gave it a try. It worked for them, and soon we were all set to go.

I gazed into the ocean towards where Marissa was pointing.

"That's our path? That's deep."

I turned and looked back at the others.

I wondered what we would find in our destination, the darkest cave in the ocean.

And what did the rest of Faith's Friendship clue mean?

And how would we handle Slate if he attacked?

Marissa started down into the crevice on the ocean floor that led to an open reef.

I stored my wandering thoughts away and followed without hesitation.

Chapter 4

THE OCEAN'S BLUE WONDER

After eating the delicious Breath of the Sea flower, my friends and I were gazing into the blue wonder of the amazing ocean.

Marissa indicated us to follow her.

And with a flick of her tail, she was shooting down towards the coral reef by the crevice.

I gave a small nod to the others behind me and paddled after Marissa, Faith hot on my trail.

The faint sunlight shone through the water and onto the soft sandy seafloor. Manta rays glided underneath us, as if flying underwater.

Sea urchins covered the sandy grounds and their purple color illuminated a pufferfish, who was busy deflating after a scare.

As we approached, it quickly ducked in the cover of the colorful coral reef.

Few schools of Hawaiian Racoon butterfish swam in the clear blue water and raced each other, though they looked alarmed as they twisted in the water.

Clownfish darted in and out of pink flowery sea anemones, swooping in the seaweed. They too looked distracted as they swam around. I glanced around and realized those were the only fish in sight.

"Hello!" Buttercup poked at a nearby dolphin. "What's your name?"

The dolphin grunted in surprise. "Go away, kid. I'm busy protecting my pod!" the dolphin clicked at her. "Scram, fish-face!"

"Oh. Sorry for disturbing you." Buttercup paddled to Lily's side. "Why don't dolphins like to talk to Buttercup? Do they not like Buttercup? Buttercup wonder why they are cranky."

"Don't worry about that, Buttercup," Lily told her. "The dolphin said he was busy."

"Don't worry, it's not your fault." I chimed in. "Some weird things have been going on here, and the animals are alert."

Buttercup nodded knowledgeably, drooping slightly.

She brightened and darted down and picked six small sea flowers, then handed them out to us.

"For you!" Buttercup chirped sweetly, handing me a purple flower before paddling to the others. "Buttercup think this will be a lucky charm and help you save Friendship!"

She grabbed another flower and taste-tested it, sticking her tongue inside to grab nectar. "Yum!"

"Thank you!" I exclaimed, swimming slower. I observed the lack of happiness in the surrounding creatures.

Green sea turtles half-heartedly nibbled sea sponges while Monk seals swam on their backs, every few seconds looking around.

As we swam deeper, no fish darted between kelp patches, and no Clown fish played in the anemones.

A tough-looking tiger shark patrolled the deeper waters looking warily at us.

As we swam even deeper, I didn't see any more creatures.

I shivered in the water, realizing it was getting colder as we dove deeper.

Buttercup busied herself making a bracelet for Lily using kelp and thin strands of embroidery. She weaved the kelp with tiny, nimble fingers.

If we could save Friendship, Buttercup would be able to play in harmony with the animals, with not a care in the world.

"Where's all the fish gone?" I caught up with Marissa. "Earlier I didn't see any! And there should still be some creatures down here. Did they vacate these premises?"

"I'm not sure." Marissa shrugged. "All I know is that fish have been disappearing rapidly! Their numbers have dropped."

The loss of fish would make a big impact on everyone in the ocean, I thought.

We swam into another crevice in the ground and went deeper. I gulped. The Breath of the Sea flower didn't make me confident in swimming and diving in deep waters.

I mean, I can float and tread, but in big waves? Definitely not! And we were going even deeper!

"This is the darkest cave in all of Maui." Marissa slowed to a halt. In front of her stood the darkest cave in the ocean.

Shadows hung from the walls and a gust of water blew by the cave's opening.

Buttercup was whining loudly. "Buttercup don't want to go down there! It is creepy and scary, and, and, and...."

"Buttercup." Lily gently blinked at her pixie. "We are doing this to save Friendship. It's your decision. Do you want to enter the cave?"

Buttercup hesitated.

"She can stay with us for a while," Marissa suggested. "Emily wants to show Buttercup what Sea Star sorbet tastes like. Or she could taste-test other treats, like iced cream."

"Yum!" Buttercup drooled.

"Buttercup don't know what that tastes like, but Buttercup think it tastes good, probably!"

"How do you eat ice cream underwater?" Olivia asked.

"It's iced. The iced cream doesn't dissolve underwater." Marissa informed her.

"Now, Buttercup! Your decision?"

Buttercup hesitated, smacking her lips. "Hard, hard, hard test! But Buttercup is no adorable, cute scared-cat, no, no, no!"

"Enter cave!" Buttercup nodded, saluting with a new expression on her face. "Save Friendship! Yay! Buttercup can do it!"

Lily smiled with approval.

A determined look was plastered on Buttercup's face.

"But that doesn't mean Buttercup don't wanna eat sorbet. Buttercup wanna have some later, ok?"

"Great. Let's go." Faith started forward.

"Do you want to come with us?" I asked Marissa.

Marissa sighed, pressing her hand against mine.

"I'd love to help you, Pia. But mermaids are forbidden to enter dark caves. This is all I can do for you."

"But," she hastily added, "I'll keep an eye out. If you need help, send Buttercup."

I smiled and thanked her as she swam away.

Turning to the cave entrance, I gulped. "Here we go."

Buttercup did a raspberry at the underwater spider webs on the cave walls.

Taking the nectar jug, she inhaled deeply and drank more nectar.

Lily nudged Buttercup forward, Faith, Olivia and I following.

We entered the dark cave.

There was no going back.

We were officially on our own.

Chapter 5

COMMANDER CRUSHER'S MISSION

Commander Crusher glared as his targets, the Friendship fairies, entered the dark cave with a tiny pixie.

His leg scraped a rock.

Slate had used dark magic to shrink Crusher for this important spy mission so the fairies wouldn't spot them so easily.

Slate needed fresh information about the fairies, and where they were traveling to, and the perfect time to ambush them and take their Friendship stones.

With a wave of his leg, Crusher signaled his other spiders, who were also shrunken, to follow him before darting into the cave.

The Breath of the Sea flower Crusher and his spiders had chomped down was sweet and tangy, and Commander Crusher detested it.

Yet Commander Crusher felt nervous swimming around.

He knew why.

Spiders were not meant to swim. They were meant to drown in the ocean, yet here they were, alive!

Later he would report the flower to Slate, yet Crusher knew Slate wouldn't be too happy about the flower.

It was so sugary! Bleck!

Commander Crusher glanced at his surroundings. Underwater webs were draped on the walls, and fish bones lined the edges of the passage.

Crusher recognized this cave at once.

Every spider knew who lived inside.

If the fairies didn't turn back now, they were going to regret it.

His leg hairs tingled in the water, tracing movement ahead.

Commander Crusher cocked his head and turned to his spiders. "Get behind a fish bone! They're coming!"

Chapter 6
THE DARKEST DOOM

Wilted kelp hung of the cave walls.

The ground was dirty and fish bones lined the edges.

My friends and I glided through the dark cave, looking around for Faith's Friendship stone.

Faith shivered, and I realized with a jolt it was freezing. We soon had swum so far, that the light from the opening could not reach us.

Buttercup emitted enough light so we could see each other.

My wings wrapped around me like a coat. I whirled around.

I could feel tiny eyes boring into my back. I could swear I heard a small whisper.

Lily sneezed suddenly, bumping Buttercup.

Buttercup tumbled into the Wina in Lily's hand. She didn't emerge and I guessed the little pixie was dazed from the fall.

Olivia handed Lily a handkerchief.

But we had not gone any further when two fairies stepped from the shadows.

One held a small lantern that illuminated the tight space.

They were each decked with deadly pistols, and one had a long sword that was covered in blood, as if they had recently been through a sword fight.

The fairy that was holding the lantern had long golden hair, and the other one had brown hair. Both fairy's hair was frizzled, as if they had been zapped by lightning.

The fairy with gold hair wore a tattered yet deathly looking dress that seemed to swallow the lantern light whole.

Their wings were skinny and black on the edges, as if they had been burnt in a pathway of raging fire.

PIRATES!

Cursed pirate fairies!

Cursed Pirate fairies were cursed to be underwater forever in the darkness of the cave.

"Hello, my dear friends." Hissed the golden-haired pirate, bunching her fists. "My name is Gold. And this is Bronze." She motioned towards the other pirate.

"What brings you here to Darkest Doom cave?" Both figures slinked forward like snakes.

My feet tapped lightly on the floor of the cave.

"We are only passing by. That does no harm, does it?" I retorted to them. I knew the pirate fairies were a dangerous group, and it was not good to be soft with them.

"I sure wonder who put all these fish bones here. Yours?"

I pointed to the sides of the cave, which many scattered bones lined.

Behind me, I felt Faith stiffen.

"Avast me hearties! Don't get us wrong. We don't care about fish. We only need it to feed our little pets, though the fish bones are fabulous decoration, we have to admit that." Smiled Bronze evilly, showing rotten yellowed teeth.

Gold narrowed her eyes, inspecting us.

"Hmm…… Friendship fairies? Aren't you looking for your petty little stones?"

"That is not your business." I said, keeping my cool.

"Moody." Huffed Gold. "I'm hurt by your words."

"We are simply here, I repeat, to perhaps pass through?"

"I don't believe you." Growled Bronze, her hair blowing ominously with the current.

"Lock them up!" Gold roared, pointing at us.

Before my friends could react, from behind Gold sprang dark shapes that whizzed around us so fast a chilly current gusted into me.

I gasped and sent a water bubble at one of the creatures in defense as quickly as I could. The creature was too fast and I missed.

Faith and the others did the same, but the creatures dodged them with ease.

I got a look up close at the creature swimming past me.

It was a shadow monster!

Shadow monsters originated from shadows, yet when a stray strand of magic landed on a shadow, it filled it with life.

And it became known as a shadow monster.

Shadow monsters could form any dark shape they wanted, and they worked with cursed pirate fairies.

"HEY!" Olivia yelled as a Shadow monster lifted her up and pinned her arms to her waist.

A second monster held down her thrashing legs and trapped her on the cold ground.

Her wings unraveled around her and took a hit at the shadow monster desperately, but the monster didn't even flinch.

I rushed to her side and pried the great shadow monster off her while Faith and Lily formed a protective circle.

The shadow monster moaned as I whammed into it.

Then with Olivia helping, we threw it at the pirates who were perfecting their evil laughs.

I puffed up my wings, making me look bigger and fiercer.

I joined Faith and Lily in the protective circle, fending off approaching monsters.

"Get off!" Lily screamed. I did a double-take as four monsters jumped on her, pinning her to the ground and separating her from the circle.

"Watch out!" I breathed to Faith. Olivia took hits at the shadow monsters on Lily.

There was a whizz of water as Faith launched a water bubble at attackers and I rushed over to defend my friend.

A shadow monster galloped forward, aiming for Faith.

I quickly threw myself in front of Faith and took a blow to the side.

Feeling woozy, I shot a water bubble at the shadow monster and it fled.

"Pia!" Faith stammered, and I whipped around.

She was cornered by a large group of shadow monsters.

The shadow monsters lunged forward.

I swam over and shot water bubbles, trying to divert their attention, but the shadow monsters ignored me.

They carried Faith on their backs and slammed her against the wall.

"NO!" I yelled. "STOP! Faith!"

Faith sagged down to the ground, unconscious. Blood streamed from a cut on her cheek.

"FAITH!" I screamed.

My heart thudded in my ears. I quickly dodged as a shadow monster lunged at me.

It crashed into the wall.

Olivia was coughing hard and was covered in dust, her cheek bruised. A pair of monsters rushed over and pinned her to the ground.

A trio of shadow monsters held Lily by the waist and as she struggled, they tightened their grip.

No. No! NO!

I rushed to Lily's side, but the shadow monsters threw me towards Gold, who was holding the lantern.

Gold stopped mid-laugh and pulled an old rusty pirate pistol from her belt.

I knocked it away with my right hand.

"It's no use!" Gold bellowed as Bronze dragged me off. They didn't bother to retrieve their barnacle-covered pistol.

I attempted to swim over to Olivia, but a monster gripped my leg and pulled me back.

I formed a water bubble and thrust it at the monster, which collided with a splash. It stumbled back and another shadow monster took its place.

The monster growled and formed into a bull shark. The bull shark gave a sharp jab with one fin and twisted my leg horridly with its teeth.

I inhaled sharply.

My hands felt numb as I fingered for my pocket knife, with no energy for a water bubble. I felt the handle and fought for the energy to pull it out.

My leg felt hot. My world turned hazy.

The bull shark sunk its teeth in deeper, as if trying to rip my skin.

I couldn't bear watch and tore my gaze away from my leg. I let go of my pocket knife, which slipped back inside the case.

I fell onto a shadow monster and rolled again and again, tussling with it.

It yanked my left wing and I kicked it with my good leg, as if to say, "That'll teach you to mess with me!"

The other Shadow monsters galloped over and threw me against the cave walls.

The fish bones scattered at my impact, and I gasped as dust invaded my lungs.

I coughed it out and heard my voice grow hoarse.

I glimpsed Olivia and Lily, and saw their faces were pressed into the ground, muffling their frantic pleas for help.

Then I saw the two pirates, golden and brown-haired glaring at me with a look of hate and triumph.

Darkness overwhelmed me, I gave in to the dizziness as everything went black.

Chapter 7
CAPTURED BY PIRATES!

Worried voices filled my ears.

"Pia. Please wake up!" A voice urged, and a gentle hand rubbed my shoulder. "Pia!"

I hazily forced myself into consciousness, feeling the cool waves of the ocean brush my cheek.

Slowly I sat up and realized with a jolt that my leg was searing hot with pain.

I stopped myself from moaning and cleared my foggy head, looking around. I was sitting in a cell covered in algae and black kelp.

A handkerchief was wrapped around my poor leg, but streaks of scarlet were still visible, coming out of the wrap.

I realized the voices who had called me were none other than my friends', Olivia, and Lily, kneeling next to me.

I winced sharply. My head pounded.

I felt paralyzed, like every bone in my body, every sensation, tingle of magic had just drained out of me.

"Are you okay?" Lily leaned forward to look at my leg.

"Olivia! Lily!" I breathed, relieved that I wasn't alone.

"Was I sleeping? Or did I pass out?"

"Sure looked like it. But we needed to check." Lily answered.

I limply sat there.

"Where's Faith?"

The question hung there.

Silence.

"T-t-the pirates took her up for questioning." Olivia shook her head sadly, glanced up at the ceiling and shuddered.

Lily looked down.

"The pirates made a threat; if Faith dies under questioning, they would take one of us next," Lily finished.

"WHAT??? FAITH!" gasping, I pounded against the bars of the cage we were imprisoned in.

Olivia and Lily looked at me feebly through exhausted eyes.

"We've already tried breaking out." Olivia whispered softly, collapsing on the kelp.

"It's no use. They used dark magic to create the bars. We're stuck."

"NO!" I cried and pressed my face to the evil bars of the dark and gloomy dungeon.

"I am NOT losing Faith!" I twirled a water bubble on my finger and pressed it into a tight ball.

I was determined to get out and save Faith, and NO ONE was going to stop me.

"She's my friend! Friends don't let friends d-d-die..."

My leg was screeching in agony, but I ignored it. Pain flooded my veins, and I banged the bars.

This was for Faith! I struck the bars.

And Olivia and Lily. No one should deserve to live in this dump of a dungeon, especially not my friends.

I swayed on my feet but pushed up in return and hurled my water bubble.

For Faith. Olivia, Lily.

My breathing was growing ragged, and for a second, I could hear only myself.

For Faith. And my dear, loyal friends.

It felt like years had passed with me standing, struggling to break out.

I would not lose Faith. Or anyone else.

"Come on, help me." I urged Olivia and Lily.

It took strength just to talk.

My throat was terribly sore. My speech came out in hoarse coughs, croaks, and gasps of breath.

"If we all make a water bubble and use the pressure of the water to squeeze it together with more water force, we might be able to blast our way out of here."

The water bubble was used for defense, but could it break our cell bars?

Olivia stood up on shaking legs. "It's worth a try. We'll be stronger with three fairies."

Lily stumbled over, and on my order, we hurled three water bubbles at the bars.

The water bubbles went through and smashed into the walls.

The bars remained unharmed.

"What?" Lily exclaimed in dismay, squinting her eyes at the bar. "The bars don't even carry a single scratch!"

We tried many more times, but with no success. I glared at the dungeon bars.

I almost wished there was a padlock. Then I could probably pick open the lock with something.

"It's too much!" Olivia wailed. "We'll never get out of here!" Her eyes drooped.

"How is my leg?" I asked Lily, changing the topic. "I can't bear to look!"

Lily opened the handkerchief slightly, and I suppressed a scream of pain. "Bad."

With nothing better to do, I pulled out my pocket knife and hit the bars with it desperately.

But it was no use. Slipping the knife back into my pocket, I sighed and racked my brain.

My injury I would deal with later.

It wasn't as important as Faith.

But did we have any means of communication with the outside world?

Lily seemed to read my thoughts and dug around in her Wing-on.

She pulled the Wina out, along with a large jug of nectar. I sat up.

"I can ask Buttercup for help." Lily grinned.

"Great!" Olivia exclaimed.

"Buttercup needs to be fed nectar often, being a small pixie," Lily explained. "But as she gets older, she'll master her magic and consume less nectar."

Olivia seemed to glow with hope and I cheered.

"Buttercup! You in there?" Lily called into the Wina. "I need you to go send for help. I have a lot of nectar!"

No response.

Olivia edged closer to the Wina. "Buttercup? Buttercup?"

"Buttercup reporting to duty." Came a small whisper. A thin Buttercup struggled out of the Wina and onto Lily's hand.

She was even smaller than ever, and her frilly hula skirt hung loosely around her waist.

Her pixie hat was lopsided on her head and her bright red hair had lost its color. "Miss Lily..."

"Buttercup!" Lily wailed. "What happened to you?"

"Negative energy." Buttercup sighed meekly, collapsing on Lily's hand.

"Are you strong enough to call for help?" Lily wondered, stroking Buttercup's hair with her finger. "Or do you need any nectar? You'll be fine, Buttercup, I know you will."

Lily pulled out the nectar jug and Buttercup gulped it down, looking like an alley cat searching for scraps.

"Save F-friendship... Butter-cup-try-Miss." Buttercup whispered. She stood up.

"Buttercup will save you, Buttercup... Will call for help... Will try to help......"

Buttercup swam forward to the dungeon bars.

At once she was repelled backward, yet she swam forward again. "Buttercup WILL... save friends."

Buttercup gasped, and she lifted her arms.

A hazy smoke drifted from Buttercup's head.

"You can't win." A voice hissed, and a wave of black swirled around Buttercup.

Dark magic!

"Butter-cup can!" Buttercup mustered up her remaining ounces of strength.

Her small hands formed a pink shimmering orb. She thrust it at the bars.

It burst.

There was a crackle like thunder as a whirlpool appeared, spinning violently around Buttercup.

It was dark and pitch-black as the sky at night, and it emitted a strong sense of negative, dark energy.

"Oh!" Buttercup struggled and swam forward desperately to escape.

"BUTTERCUP!" Lily yelled, swimming forward to reach her pixie. She was thrown back by the powerful magic.

She collided into the wall.

"BUTTERCUP!"

Buttercup's hula skirt was ripping.

Buttercup turned around and hurled pink orbs at the whirlpool.

POOF!

The whirlpool vanished in the blink of the eye.

The bars to the dungeon seemed to lash out at Buttercup, who let out a squeak of surprise before being hurled at the dungeon walls.

"Buttercup!" Olivia, Lily and I screamed, though we were glued to the wall, unable to help.

My leg was bleeding again, though I didn't care. "Buttercup!"

Buttercup got up and glared at the bars of the dungeon.

Her hair set on fire as she stumbled forward. "Buttercup...will save..."

Buttercup ducked as a whirl of black shot at her. "Friends!"

The wave of black doubled back.

It came up behind her and formed into an orb that started to encase Buttercup.

I stared in shock as Buttercup wailed softly, and weakly kicked the orb around her.

I saw a limp body before the orb obscured my vision.

BOOM!

My friends stepped back in horror. Seaweed and kelp whirled around in the water and shot in all directions.

I ducked as the seaweed approached and screeched in pain as some kelp slapped my leg.

The seaweed and kelp settled down, and a fresh wave of cold water spread over me, coming from Buttercup's direction.

But suddenly the moving water seemed to turn into ice.

I opened my eyes, wiping grime from my face.

A lifeless Buttercup lay limp in Lily's hand.

"BUTTERCUP!" Lily screamed, laying the small pixie on the ground.

She tapped Buttercup gently with a finger, but the pixie budged no more. "Buttercup?"

"No! No! No! BUTTERCUP!" Lily sobbed. She kneeled on the ground.

"No…. It wasn't your time! BUTTERCUP!"

"No…" Olivia and I sat down miserably.

Tears pooled in the water, and I hugged Lily.

She toppled over onto the ground next to Buttercup's body, weeping.

"Buttercup! NO!"

Lily gasped, covering Buttercup's body with a beautiful satin handkerchief. "Buttercup…"

Lily's eyes swelled puffy and red, and I patted Lily's back.

Olivia broke out crying too, clawing at her own face until red marks could be seen.

"Buttercup." I choked. Tears trickled down my cheek.

I had not known young Buttercup for long, but I already valued her like I valued all my very good friends.

It was not meant to be. The darkness in our cell wrapped around me so tight I hardly dared breath.

I moved the Wina next to Buttercup's body, so Buttercup's home would be beside her always.

The Wina had turned a puking green, and the wings flapped, then shriveled into dust.

There was a shimmer of golden sparkles, and the Wina and Buttercup's body was dissolving before us.

The sparkles tailed out the dungeon bars.

"Buttercup's wings sparkled like that." Lily whispered, following the sparkles to the bars of the cage.

Buttercup was gone.

Forever.

I gripped the bars of the dungeon even tighter, willing them to break.

If we didn't try to escape, we would be here forever. We needed stamina to escape.

"We will escape for Buttercup and for Faith." I gritted my teeth.

My fingers gripped tightly around the bars and I willed myself to think through my dizziness and blurry mind.

An earsplitting shriek echoed above me.

"Please! NO!" A strangled voice sounded far off in the distance.

It was Faith.

"Just let them go! Don't hurt them!" Faith shrieked.

I could feel her pain, her loyalty.

"If you let them go, I'll stay here in their place! I'll do anything!"

Faith… loyal Faith.

"Tell me, what are you doing here with your comrades?" A dark voice hissed. "You WILL tell me! If you don't, I swear I will…"

I didn't hear the rest.

A warm sensation tickled me, and I looked up to find a strand of glowing yarn connecting me too… Faith!

I could suddenly see her, Faith, and the Pirates.

They were standing right next to Faith, holding a knife to her throat, surrounded by shadow monsters.

Faith's eyes were focused on the tip of the knife, and she was barely breathing, though she looked petrified.

I remembered what a good friend Faith had been to me, and I knew I would not let those evil pirates torture her.

They would not touch her at all.

The vision disappeared.

Instantly my hands swiftly moved in a circle shape, as if tracing a ball.

I felt warm, like sipping hot cocoa on a cold, snowy day.

Sparkles emerged from deep inside me, it gave me warmth and strength.

Energy.

I did not feel much pain of my injured leg.

In fact, it was healing quickly.

I watched in awe at it, as it did its wonderful work.

Scarlet streaks were no more, the wrapped handkerchief was not needed.

The fabric unraveled itself from my leg, floated for a second, then dropped to the ground.

I glanced down at my leg and flexed it.

Olivia and Lily stood up, dusting themselves off.

Olivia looked at me, her eyes fixed on my leg.

A small smile had started on Lily's gloomy face, hope.

I rose up in the water, and my skin shimmered and tingled with energy.

I lit up the darkened and gloomy dungeon cell, with the power of light and something else.

Friendship.

"For Buttercup and Faith," I whispered.

"Faith. We're coming to save you."

And then like the shining sun, a streak of light fired towards the bars, thrust from my fingertips.

The light made contact with the dungeon bars.

There was a flash and the whole dungeon shook.

The bars burst.

The dark, gloomy, dungeon was no more.

Chapter 8
THE SECRET OF FRIENDSHIP

I stared.

The dark dungeon where I had recently blasted with my newly discovered energy was no more.

Questions swarmed in my head.

How did I create the energy?

How did my leg heal so quickly?

Where did that sudden surge of magic come from?

Was it because of my Friendship talent?

Was the legend true for Friendship fairies? That we had very strong Friendship magic?

Well, rock talent fairies could use rocks to hit things. Like air, the force of nature. But rock was physical.

Friendship was different. There was a bit in everyone. You just had to find it, and it was invisible. If you turned bad, that friendship magic went somewhere else where it would be used.

You don't need to be a Friendship fairy to make friends.

You don't even need magic.

You just need courage, a bit of kindness, and a smile to become friends with someone. But once you are friends, you need to care for your friend, help them, as they would do to you.

Friendship is awesome.

But there are many mysteries about Friendship. Friendship seems very simple.

Really, it's not.

There are also many myths and poems about friendship that might be true.

Well, there was one myth and poem about friendship that went like…

Where there's friendship,
There is a dark side.
For those of pure heart,
For those who treasure,

For those who think Friendship is beyond measure,
There is a power deep within.
It cannot be abused,
It is not bat and ball,
It is only for those who are so true,
Who wishes, wants, with all their heart,
To treat their friend, to have a friend,
With the magic of Friendship.

But it was just a nursery poem, wasn't it?

"Pia?" Olivia whispered, snapping me out of my thoughts.

Her eyes were wide, and her wings were slowly wrapping themselves into a skirt.

Lily looked no different. Her mouth hung open and she was squeezing a nectar jug.

Still in a daze, I looked at myself fully, inspecting every part.

No more sparkles burst from deep inside, and no more light emitted from me.

My leg looked good, and the scar was barely visible.

"We're free?" I said, still confused by my leg and how Friendship magic had healed it.

"Let's go find Faith!" Olivia and Lily cheered, then paused.

"We can't get caught again!" Lily whispered. "Now we have to be careful. For Buttercup! And Faith!"

We silently swam alongside the passage, slipping around in the corners of the hallway and scanning the clearings ahead of us.

Slurp!

I stopped and looked around, trying to pinpoint the location of the sound.

Olivia and Lily stopped beside me.

Around the corner sat many shadow monsters sucking on metal straws.

"Look!" I whisper-shouted, pointing to a room at the side of the passage.

Mashed-up fish were kept in a container that the shadow monsters slurped on from many metallic straws.

That was where all the fish had gone!

On the side of one of the containers, I read a label, "Fish food for Pet Monsters! P.S. don't forget to close the lid!" except that it was scrawled in pirate handwriting and badly misspelled.

This was how the pirates had spelled it:

Fsh Fods fer pete moonsterks! Pee.S. don't ferget too clooss d lidd!

"This must be where the shadow monsters get their energy. And the pirates have horrible spelling skills!" I concluded, carefully peeking around the curb.

There was a stack of reed newspapers in front of me. I guessed the pirates had nabbed them from local mermaids.

One newspaper heading caught my attention. I nudged Olivia and Lily, showing them the paper. This was what it looked like:

Flying Fairies

Slate's New Commander

On the exact day the Friendship fairies were due to find their stones, Slate of Chaos appointed a new commander, Commander Crusher. A difference from the rest of Slate's commanders, Crusher is big, burly, and strong.

You don't want to mess with Commander Crusher. Crusher had trained his leg hairs to pick up movement and is determined to lead his superior to victory. All in an attempt to demolish Friendship and let darkness flood the world.

"I don't sit and plan," Commander Crusher declares to nervous reporters. "I just do it, and with brain and brawn like mine, Friendship is done for! Friendship fairies should just give up!"

Slate was not present at the time, but we are currently working on getting a brave enough reporter to interview him, one reporter who hasn't been fed to Slate's goblin sharks yet.

When asked what he intends his next move to be, Commander Crusher responded by clearing his throat and saying, "Take the Friendship stones and give them to my master, Slate of Chaos."

"Oh, my," Olivia whispered after she finished reading. "Oh no."

Lily moaned softly. "Great. One trouble after another."

"This is called adventuring and saving Maui and Friendship from Slate." I managed a weak smile. "Even Slate's so-called puny commander before Crusher was hard to deal with. Fluttering fairies!"

"Fluttering Fairies!" Lily wailed, and Olivia repeated it too, looking grim.

"We must be persistent." I insisted. "Gather your stamina. Collect your grit. We must have stamina and grit. You're my friends, and I believe we can do it."

"Yes." Lily closed her eyes. "Grit."

"Stamina," added Olivia. "We will do this."

We swam silently around the shadow monsters, careful not to stir up any bubbles.

I sighed as we made it safely across and wondered if it would be that easy to save Faith.

Lily was right. We were dealing with one trouble after another.

But the thought of Faith and the knife to her throat made my insides do a flip.

What if we were too late?

I would NEVER forgive myself. Faith would not end up like poor Buttercup.

I churned my legs and willed them to go faster.

Faith's life was at stake!

Chapter 9
COMMANDER CRUSHER'S SECRET

Commander Crusher saw it all.

He had followed the fairies out of the dungeon and to the stack of newspapers by the shadow monster feeding area.

Those fairies had finally seen the news article about him.

And they had been scared of him! Ha!

But Commander Crusher didn't like their "stamina" and "grit".

Foolish fairies.

From his own experience, he knew it was one thing to say something, and another thing to do, or be it.

His spiders were busy glancing around for the pirate's shadow monsters. Crusher stepped forward.

He, as well as Slate, didn't like the pirates. Whenever someone mentioned the word "pirate", Slate would spit furiously and send them to the Whirling waters.

So it was almost instinct that the spiders in Slate's giant spider army never said the word "pirate", or anything to so with it, like, "Loot!" or "Avast me Hearties!".

This including "Land HO!" and "Polly Parrot wants a cracker, SQUAWK!". But Commander Crusher knew pirate parrots never said those ridiculous lines.

Those feather-faces thought they were too dignified. And in the first place, not all cursed pirates had cursed parrots, did they?

Earlier, Commander Crusher had placed a shiny silver key in another dungeon on orders from Slate.

Slate had told him that the key had been cursed to work against the fairies and Crusher was eager to see it in action.

If the fairies escaped from those measly pirates and the key's magic failed to stop them, then Crusher would contact Slate so Slate could launch his evil plan.

So far, following the fairies was easy.

Crusher thought some more.

He didn't care why the pixie had died in the cell.

But what was the mysterious power that the Pia fairy unleashed? It seemed to be quite strong to break through dark magic created bars.

Crusher frowned, clamping his jaws on a stray splinter of wood. It seemed like concern for friends fueled the Pia fairy's energy.

That meant the Pia fairy might be able to raise her power and would be able to destroy anything – if she could control it.

Such great power was demanding and scary, and Crusher shivered for the first time at the thought. If that fairy used that power against him and his spider army, what was to happen?

Should Crusher warn Slate now?

Crusher hesitated and shook the thought away.

Slate would take the knowledge without giving Crusher any reward and dismiss Commander Crusher as if he was nothing more than a scrap of dirt.

The fairies were moving on, and Crusher scuttled forward to keep up, hating his small form.

Chapter 10

A CLOSE CALL

Olivia, Lily, and I swam up to a gate, kicked it open, and passed through.

After we had escaped from the dark and gloomy dungeon cell, we had found out why the fish in Maui were disappearing.

The shadow monsters mushed fish into pulp and slurped it up through straws. I felt nauseous.

And the new worry, that Slate had appointed a burly spider named Crusher to be his new commander.

Lily was whispering rapidly to Olivia, but I paid no attention.

I guessed they were probably discussing the ancient Friendship myth, and its connection to my sudden powerful Friendship energy, the shadow monsters, or Commander Crusher.

I too was wondering, but this was not the time.

My mind could only think of Faith, and poor Buttercup's tragic end.

We swam for a while more, and I hurriedly spread out my wings.

We turned another corner.

"Look!" Olivia pointed to a shadow monster on guard. "Not all of them are taking a break!"

"Oh my!" Lily exclaimed, taking in the scene.

But she said that a LITTLE too loudly.

The shadow monster then grunted and adjusted its treading position.

It formed into a large bull shark, with a narrow jaw and black streaks on its head. It had small stripe-like spots on its side, but you could still see parts of the black shadow monster by its black-tipped fins.

I clasped a hand over Lily's mouth and pulled Olivia to the side of the coral passageway. The stench of dead fish and seaweed filled my nostrils.

"If you don't be quiet, we'll be pulp." I moaned quietly to Lily. "What should we do?"

"I think we should sneak under the shark." Olivia proclaimed. Her eyes widened and she lowered her voice. "It probably won't notice us."

Lily and I cocked our heads. "Perhaps…" I said slowly, sorting out the options. "But it's also very risky."

"Alright! Let's do it!" Olivia exclaimed, standing up. In two swift moves, Lily and I pulled her down and covered her mouth.

"Shh!" we shushed Olivia, and Lily squinted her eyes worriedly, trembling. Olivia gave us an apologetic shrug.

The shark was very brawn; if we startled it we would be in trouble. And I didn't want to be mushed fairy cake.

"The longer we wait we have more time to collect fear." I declared wisely. "Let's just get on with it."

"Let's do it." Olivia declared, agreeing with me, and this time she remembered to lower her voice.

I did a short nod. "For Faith and Buttercup. We have the grit to keep going."

"For Faith." Olivia echoed and nodded, while Lily's gaze wandered away.

"For Buttercup and Faith." Lily closed her eyes as we started up. "We will save Friendship."

Olivia shot forward and swam under the shark silently, and I followed, dreading what could happen.

Lily's eyes widened.

She took a small timid breath and followed us. But halfway under the shark, she rolled over while swimming and took a glance at the bull shark's jagged teeth.

As she flipped over, a loose strand of her long blond hair seemed to reach out to the shark.

Olivia was already on the other side of the shark, and as she watched Lily, she swayed in the water in horror.

I froze.

I gasped silently, swam back, pulled Lily's hair down so it wouldn't alert the shark, and tugged her forward to the other side of the shark.

"Oh, I'm so clumsy!" Lily wailed in an undertone once we had gotten to safety, out of earshot and sight of the bull shark.

"It's okay." I comforted her. "It's okay."

We trod the water for a minute, thinking.

We had to hurry, and suddenly the urgency hit me like a wave.

"Let's go save Faith!"

Chapter 11
THE CURSED KEY

After passing the bull shark, my patience to save Faith was quickly shortening.

We had to hurry!

And besides, Faith still needed her Friendship stone to revive Friendship and defeat Slate.

But so far, there was mysteriously no sign of Slate.

Slate could be somewhere in Maui, hiding and waiting for the perfect moment to eliminate Friendship once and for all.

Was he plotting one of his evil schemes?

Or had he truly given up?

I pulled my hair in distress and gritted my teeth.

So many things were happening all at once, and I felt like I was a rock, still in time, while events blurred past me.

And to add to our problem pile, there were so many threats and obstacles in our way. Like Commander Crusher, the huge spider which could pick up movement with his leg hair.

I sighed, pulling myself together.

We were in this together, and we would accomplish our mission with stamina and grit.

And Friendship.

"Stop!" Lily shushed us.

We were swimming in the direction of Faith's weakening screams, and Lily was holding us back.

"What is it?" I asked impatiently, then bit my lip. We only had a bit more to go before we found Faith.

"Look!" Lily swam around the next corner. "There's Faith!"

I followed her and saw Faith.

Her hands were cuffed, and as I had thought, the pirates held a sword or some type of dagger to her neck that forced Faith to kneel down.

I recognized the two pirates - gold-haired Gold and brown-haired Bronze as they towered over Faith.

Faith let out a strangled breath and collapsed onto the ground in front of a huge pirate ship.

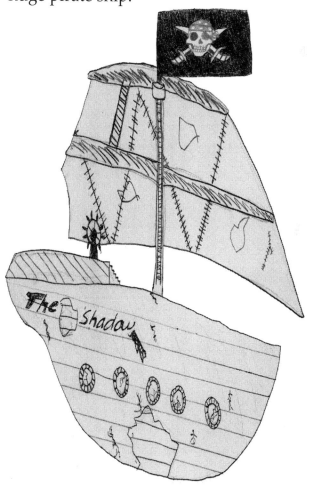

A row of shadow monsters swam around them, each one a different underwater creature.

I spotted a giant box jellyfish floating nearby and recoiled with a shudder.

The box jellyfish is known to be highly venomous. Their poison can consume you, flesh and bone, within minutes!

"TELL ME!" bellowed Gold. "Where do you keep your precious Friendship stones?"

Faith didn't answer. I was glad her Friendship stone was safely stowed in her Wing-on.

"TELL ME." Gold stared at Faith. "I hear your Friendship stones are quite valuable, eh? How much gold would Slate of Chaos give us in exchange for all three Friendship stones? ALONG with three Friendship fairies and an outsider?"

"NO!" Faith cried, trembling all over. "Friendship stones are for Friendship! Not for you mangy pirates to sell!"

"TELL ME NOW!" Gold hissed, spitting in Faith's face.

Faith stuck her tongue out and turned away from the filthy pirate.

"Bring the other scallywags here!" Bronze shrieked at a nearby shadow monster. "Will you give us the Friendship stones, or would you watch your friends die?"

Faith shuddered and didn't say anything else.

A shadow monster transformed into a thresher shark swam by, heading for the cells with jagged teeth.

I felt a tug, and next thing I knew, Lily had pulled Olivia and me into a nearby room.

I was buried in anger. That Gold deserved to be copper! No, wait, coal!

My head felt hot.

I gritted my teeth to stop myself from zooming straight into Gold and Bronze, and their shadowy crew.

Bubbles whirled around, my legs churned, and suddenly my fists were clenched.

My patience was bubbling, like lava erupting to the brim of a volcano.

The lava only grew inside of me. I was ready to kick that shadow monster!

"Ugh!" I groaned, the noise muffled by Lily's handkerchief as she held it over my face. "Let go!" Olivia and Lily were restraining me, as I tried to swim to Faith.

"I…"

"…need…"

"…to…"

I struggled again. "Go save Faith!"

And maybe I wasn't thinking it that time, but a minute after I realized it was a good thing Olivia and Lily had hauled me into a room far from the pirates.

"Pia!" Lily gasped, panting. "We have to slow down! Your desperation is clouding over your wits!"

I thought it over in my head but cleared it away.

By then I had stopped struggling, and now Olivia and Lily now had a very firm grip on me.

"But! FAITH!" I wailed, pulling on my hair. "I can't leave her back there!"

"Uh, hello?"

A quavering voice whimpered.

Olivia and Lily released my legs.

We all turned around, to see a young mermaid. She was locked in a cell. Heavy metal chains were draped on her shoulders, stranding her on the bottom of the cage.

She had purple wavy hair tied in a fishtail braid, and her tail was an elegant pink fuchsia.

"Who are you?" I asked suspiciously, swimming forward.

"I-I am Lydia, Nymph of Currents." She replied earnestly, trying to swim up. "I was captured by the pirates. Can you help me?"

"We will try our best." I said simply and placed my hand onto the cage bars.

"Pia, can you do that thing again?" Lily asked me, and I noticed worry in her eyes. I paused.

Faith…. Friendship stones…. ARGH!

Thoughts whirled in my brain. I forced myself to concentrate on what Lily was saying.

"I'm not sure," I exclaimed. "These bars are strong. Though maybe I could find a weak point in time with a little bit of stamina and grit. Everything has a weak point!"

Olivia cautiously looked around, checking for shadow monsters.

"I used my own brand of magic in an attempt to break it." Lydia sighed, swirling nearby water with a hand. "But it was too strong."

"I'm the Guardian of the Coral Maze," she stated.

"OMG!" Olivia exclaimed in pure awe, interrupting her before she could say anything else.

"You're Guardian of the Coral Maze?"

Lydia nodded, massaging her hand.

"Yes. But even if I try to summon a big current to break me out of this cell, nothing happens! My powers don't work anymore."

"That's horrible!" Lily looked at Lydia with sympathy in her eyes.

A twinkle of reflected light attracted my gaze from the far side of the room, and I could make out a small key lying on the ground.

"There's a key!" I exclaimed, and didn't wait for an answer, swimming swiftly over to the shining key. "It must be the key to your cell!"

"YES!" Lydia cheered, looking livelier than ever. "THE KEY! How did I not notice that? When I'm free, I'm going to go to my Coral Maze straight away! I love its bright red color, and how there's so much life besides it. The animals would swim around and play together in the Coral Maze, oh, they must miss me!"

Lydia squealed. "I'm so excited, I'll see my other nymph friends, they must be really worried."

"That sounds fun." I lightly picked up the key and started to swim over to the mermaid's heavy padlocked cage, getting ready to open the big padlock.

Dizziness overwhelmed me.

I paused.

I was struck by a jolt of magic, and it was like being electrified.

My hair frizzled and crackled with magic, and I jolted up and gasped, looking around.

My breath became heavier with each pant, and I felt weary as ever, darkness threatening to overwhelm me.

Clink.

The silver key clattered onto the bare floor.

"Pia?" Lily whispered. "You ok?"

My mouth moved. No sound came out.

I felt myself sink next to the key.

I stared helplessly onto the ground ahead for a dreadful moment. Then black.

I woke to the shaking of multiple hands gripping my waist.

My right hand reached instantly to my side, searching for a shining blade of silver.

That's when I opened my eyes.

"Pia!" Olivia and Lily were crouched by me, their gazes panic-stricken.

"What happened?" asked Lydia breathlessly, huffing as she collapsed under her chains.

She was staring at the key in confusion.

"I'm fine." I snapped. "Stop sticking your nose in where it doesn't belong, nymph!"

"Pia!" Lily cried, grasping my hand.

My vision blurred, the edges violent purple as I clutched the key.

Dark thoughts infiltrated my mind. If it weren't for Friendship, I wouldn't be dragged onto this wild goose chase.

What was the point?

There weren't any friends that weren't betrayed.

Betrayed...

Yes.

A voice in my head lectured.

After you find the Friendship stones with them, they will ditch you, and leave you humiliated and alone, and take all the glory.

YOUR glory.

The voice in my head continued.

But ditch them first, my dear, and join me, Slate, and you will be well respected.

You will never be alone, I am with you.

I am the KEY to your wildest dreams.

Key. Who cared about Faith?

I didn't. And what was the point in saving her? She would ditch me and leave with the others.

Key...

Dream...

Slate...

Betrayal sounded like a nice plan.

"Finally." I cackled, with a voice that was high pitched and definitely not Pia the Pinena Fairy's.

Lily edged closer. "Pia, are you okay?"

"Go away!" I sourly hissed. "You pesky fly! Anyone have a flyswatter? Because I need a giant one over here!"

Lily flinched, which gave me much satisfaction.

"Pia, are you really okay?" Olivia met blue eyes to my purple eyes. "Not, hit your-head-almost-dead or something?"

"Oh, I'm totally fine," I exclaimed cheerily. "I'm just being myself, you moron!"

Olivia glanced at Lily. "Pia? There's something different about you," Olivia began, but I cut her off.

"Oh, I'm just wondering!" I shouted at her. "Why I'm here with these freaks!"

Olivia's eyes widened, but she quickly regained her normal posture.

I straightened up and swam slowly towards Lily, who was sucking her lips together in worry.

"You're such a scaredy-cat! I wonder how your parents raised such an awful little fairy! They must be so ashamed!" I hissed. "How clumsy! You almost made fish-food out of yourself when you almost tickled that bull shark!"

Lily blinked at me and drew back.

"Pia, this isn't like you!" Olivia whined, hurt showing in her eyes.

"Yeah!" Lily croaked, sniffling. Olivia gave her a handkerchief.

"You're always so nice and kind, with many ideas! And you have many friends, not just because you're a Friendship talent fairy, it's because that's how big your heart is!"

"You're our BFF!" The two fairies exclaimed in unison.

"Don't say that word!" I growled, stalking forward. I was a tiger on a hunting mission. Or an underwater tiger.

"You just don't know." Holding a strip of kelp, I ripped it into shreds and tossed it away.

"Evil is the only thing that will survive. And once Slate has your Friendship stones, he will destroy friendship."

Olivia gasped. Lily bared her teeth.

"Oh! I forgot to add something." I smirked nastily. "Don't get in Slate's way if you would like a longer lifespan."

Lydia was petrified.

Her hands were cupped over her mouth, but it was obvious that her jaw was hanging so low, it could brush the ground.

"Slate will take over the world and be the ruler. You don't belong in his world. You are a link to Friendship." I informed them with glee.

"All Friendship fairies are done for."

"Pia!" Lily said somberly, as she turned to face me. "YOU are a friendship fairy!"

"Not anymore." My eyes narrowed into slits.

"I am the Fairy of Darkness!"

Chapter 12
THE FAIRY OF DARKNESS

Faith, Lily, and Olivia were complete, utter little brats.

I couldn't trust them.

Yes, Yes. The same voice whispered in my ear.

Destroy them, hurt them before they turn on you.

With this power the silver key gives, it will enrich you with evil.

You will learn fruitful ways to destroy friendship. Use this wisely.

I looked at the key in my hand, revolving it fully and feeling the fresh wave of its powers.

An idea popped into my evil brain.

"DEMONS!" I shrieked.

There was a burst of purple light.

Demons ascended from my outstretched palms, looking around menacing.

The demons were dark purple with night black streaks and looked almost like ghosts with their ghastly essence.

But I knew they were fiercer than they looked.

The demon's bottom tapered into a thin tip.

Their eyes were black, bottomless holes.

Their teeth were rotten yellow with dark green grim.

Their jaws were wide, and a few had overbites from biting into flesh. Blood stained their faces.

Olivia and Lily backed up, holding their noses at the demon's stench.

Evil and good have different tastes of how things should smell.

But the demon's odor was as pleasant as garbage in a wasteland to me. Personally, that smell should be the next perfume for evil-doing villains!

I grinned widely.

"Perfect." The group of demons were ready to start sucking on fear.

They were sort of like vampires.

But that was even better.

And miserable Faith I would leave to the pirates. I would encourage the demons to decide if they wanted to possess her or drink her fear.

Each demon gave a short nod and hungry grunt, waiting for me to speak.

I, the Fairy of Darkness, was now their new and evil mistress!

And this was it.

This was the end of Olivia and Lily.

On my orders, the demons would now attack Olivia and Lily and show no mercy.

A piece of cake!

Not that I could believe I once enjoyed cake! It was too creamy and tangy and I especially hated fruitcake. The fruits on it were always too – fresh.

I turned and gestured for the demons to step closer.

The demons looked eagerly at me, ready to take my orders.

"Attack th- "

I yelled, then paused.

"Actually, I have a better idea!" I rubbed my hands together.

"Let us go to Faith. She'll entertain us before she DIES right in front of her friend's eyes."

"No!" Olivia lunged onto the nearest demon.

She kicked the demon, but it clasped her in its jaws and hurled her at the wall. She caught herself just in time, though her head hit the wall and she collapsed onto a startled Lily.

The demon looked at her, sprawled onto the ground. It hissed and kicked her.

Lily helped Olivia up, who was whimpering from a large bump on her forehead.

Suddenly, sensing Olivia's fear, the demons started crowding around her.

Demons feed on fear, often leaving their victims lifeless, a shell of their former life.

The demons pushed and shoved each other, growling as if rowdy kids fighting over a lollipop.

The nearest demon opened its mouth and gave a high-pitched shriek like a dog whistle that was barely audible.

A thin strand of dark magic struck Olivia, attaching her to the demon.

Something flowed out of her.

It was her fear, mixed with her life energy.

Lily gasped in shock.

The demons started on Lily. Fear and life energy started to drain out of her.

"HELP!" Lily screamed, breaking free of the line attaching her to the demon.

She backed up to the wall as the wave of demons moved closer, showing their jagged teeth.

Lily pulled Olivia free of her line of fear, and shoved Olivia behind her, continuing to fend off the demons.

Lydia the mermaid nymph had tensed and backed up to the walls of her cage, prepared to defend herself from the demons.

"You may drink the fear and life energy of Olivia and Lily later." I decided, swimming up to the demons.

"Hurry! I can't wait to torture Faith!"

A demon grunted in a mixture of protest, whines, and starvation.

"Fine. One more minute." I giggled with glee. "Just make sure you don't drink their fear too fast. Just make them a bit helpless, okay?"

The demon licked its chapped lips and gorged on Lily, who squealed and lashed out helplessly.

"I like the thought of Olivia and Lily, the Friendship failures feeling helpless while their best friend DIES!"

The demon accepted this but stared at Lydia hungrily.

"We'll come back for the nymph later, don't fret cha' evil mind." I assured it.

"Wow, you're evil! Absolutely vicious! I like how ya think!"

I dismissed the demon and continued watching them torture Olivia and Lily.

I watched as Olivia and Lily screamed.

I saw the panic sparking in their eyes.

I could feel their pleading stares.

And I watched as Olivia and Lily slowly started to grow limp, their shoulders sagging, chests heaving in pain.

"Pia!" Lily whispered. "You in there?"

"PLEASE! HELP!" Olivia wailed.

I turned away, but something had changed about me.

My stomach started heaving and squeezing together.

My heart tightened as if trying to crush the evil within me.

Suddenly my heart burst with warmth. I inhaled sharply.

My hair levitated, just for a second.

Then it fell back on my shoulders as I exhaled.

The demons were too busy with my friends to notice me.

I saw Olivia's head loll to one side weakly.

Lily huffed raggedly.

But this felt – wrong.

A voice - a familiar one - spoke up inside me, not the evil one, but a goodhearted voice.

I will not hurt my friends! The familiar voice declared. *I will save my friends and break free from this spell!*

A voice filled with hatred and darkness protested. *Overpower the three Friendship fairies!*

If you do, Slate of Chaos will bring you great glory that friends can never give!

No. the good voice confidently exclaimed.

I don't need your glory. I need my friends! I shall vanquish you!

NOOO! The evil voice spat furiously. *This can't be! Listen, fairy! We can make a deal...*

The evil voice was quickly drowned out by the good one.

Don't even try me! The good voice warned. *I will not listen to you!*

I am Pia the Pinena Fairy! A Friendship talent fairy and loyal to my friends.

I could swear I heard a small choking sound.

I blinked.

My eyes were turning from evil purple back to a shade of dark brown.

The evil voice was fading.

Evil must win! This will not be the last you've seen of Slate of Chaos!

It rasped, then shrieked.

I blinked, and something slithered from my eyes and into the silver key.

Evil will never win!

The warm voice chanted in glory. *Friendship forever! Friendship forever!*

A fresh wave of warmth spread from my head to my toes.

Lively as ever, I felt my blood roaring as it surged into my limbs and energized me.

A new dawn was coming.

A better one.

I turned to the demons and had to contain my alarm at the sight of it.

My friends, laying helplessly on the ground.

If I didn't do anything soon…

I couldn't dread to think of what would happen to my friends!

My eyes widened, and I shook my head, trying to make the world stop spinning.

Using the handkerchief that Lily had used to bind my recently injured leg, I quickly wrapped up the key, careful not to touch it.

Then I quickly slipped it into a secret pocket in my belt.

I looked at the huge crowd of demons crowded around my friends.

There was no way I could defeat the demons, even with my friends helping.

Wait!

The demons didn't know I was good again!

I could turn it to my advantage.

I would have to be clever if I wanted to save my friends.

I had to act.

My skill in acting would decide the fate of my friends, and myself.

If the demons sensed even a minute speck of good in me, they would turn on me and we would all be doomed.

"Come." I put on my best evilly cold voice and motioned to the demons to follow me. "Your feeding time is over. Take those Friendship frauds with you, and only I, the Fairy of Darkness, will touch, er, torture them!"

The words tasted bitter on my tongue as I choked them out.

As long as the demons thought I was evil, my plan would work!

I marched-er, swam forward like I had won an award and then realized villains preferred to stalk.

I patted my pocket. The key knew that it had lost control of me, but it had no communication with the deathly demons.

For now, the key was powerless.

I tried to hunch my back - OW - but I couldn't stand too much bending. I jerked violently and straightened.

Villain wasn't for me.

"Hurry!" I thundered. If I wanted to maintain my posture, I had to yell like a mad fairy.

Which I despised.

And it hurt my throat. Ouch.

The demons picked up the pace, and I reached an intersection in the passage. Which way?

I looked around wildly, hoping for a clue. None.

The demons suddenly stopped, and a few tilted their head to the cave walls.

Bubbles streamed from them, as they searched around, looking to and fro.

"Have you - I mean, WHAT IS IT?" I boomed, glaring at them cross-eyed. "Tell-er, TELL ME, NOW!"

The demon at the very front grunted and showed gnarled teeth.

Then it hissed in the direction of one of the cave passages.

It had sensed Faith's fear.

I led the demons down the path, and pretty soon we could hear screams from Faith.

Olivia and Lily raised their heads and looked around, but were too weak to keep their heads up for long.

They slumped down as the demons carried them like mere puppets.

I hurried down the tunnel and soon came to the main opening, the demons hot on my trail.

I peeked around the corner to see Faith. The pirates were still taunting and teasing her, the shadow monsters around them grunting menacingly.

I paused, then quickly flipped back again, facing the demons.

"Listen carefully!" I growled. "I HATE those Shadow Monsters and pirates. Capture, do whatever you want to them all! But don't touch the fairy in the center, that's Faith. We'll torture her AFTER the battle, as a reward for your obedience."

The demons swished their tail-like things in anticipation.

A demon swam around Olivia and Lily, clamping its jaws together as it eyed them tastily.

Tears clouded Lily's eyes but she didn't bother to blink them away.

"I'll watch them." My eyes were fixed on Faith. "Focus on the battle. Get ready."

The demon grunted and darted to the front of the group.

Olivia and Lily hugged each other, backing away from me in fear.

I gave them a small, quick wink.

"ATTACK!"

My sudden outcry alerted the pirates, and as they turned, they gaped at the wave of demons encroaching them.

"What?" Gold gasped, fiddling with her pistol.

Before the shadow monsters could react, a pair of demons had already leaped onto each shadow monster, spitting violently.

A trio of Demons disappeared in the direction of the dungeons.

They re-emerged later, each carrying a few busted-up metal bars.

They twisted the bars together into a cage as easily as you would break a bar of chocolate.

They captured the two pirates and locked them into the cage.

The pirates fought back, and Gold pulled a pistol from her shoulder sling, firing it at the closest demon.

The bullet embedded itself in the demon's shoulder. Gold cackled.

The demon grunted in pain. Then a purple trail of magic swirled from the key in my pocket to the demon's shoulder.

There was a "Poof!" and the demon was healed. The trio left the pirates in the cage and headed back into the battle.

Gold sputtered.

I stared in shock.

But as soon as no one was watching, Olivia and Lily tugged me away from the fight scene and pinned me to the ground.

"Who are you and what have you done to our friend?" Lily shook me, lowering her voice so the demons wouldn't hear.

Her grip was weak.

Olivia glared at me.

"PERSON! FAIRY! IMPOSTER! MAGIC DUDETTE! PERSON WHO SUMMONS DEMONS TO SUCK OUR FEAR! PERSON WHO USED TO HAVE PURPLE EYES BUT NOW HAS BROWN!"

I sighed, exasperated, as Olivia and Lily exchanged a brief glance.

"Listen," I explained. "My name is Pia, and I swear that as soon as I touched the key, Slate controlled me somehow."

"That's weird. Quite a far-fetched story, but I might believe it." Olivia started, but Lily shushed her, eager to hear more.

"It must be cursed. I realized what was happening and came up with this plan. Use the demons to attack the shadow monsters, and save Faith. Please, you can trust me."

I felt Lily's grip loosen.

She was a trusting fairy, and she would believe me.

But Olivia was rock solid.

"What is your favorite candy?"

"I have a sweet tooth for sour snake candies. Do you happen to have one? One time…"

"Okay, never mind that! Um… How did you meet Faith?"

"I bumped into her at M.E. Magic Elementary. Then…"

"What is your Auntie Leona's talent?"

"What are you talking about? I don't have an Auntie Leona!"

Finally, Olivia let go of me and stood up, though she and Lily still glanced at me warily.

"Thank you." I smiled and stood up slowly at the speed rate of a snail, being careful not to spook them.

Meanwhile, the battle was still raging between the demons and shadow monsters.

Faith standing the middle of it all, looking around wildly for an escape route.

With a kick of my leg, I was in the center with Faith. Then, pulling onto her hand, I led an exhausted Faith to worried Olivia and Lily.

We embraced, but it only lasted a short time.

A triumphant yelp split the water.

I turned to see the demons staring at us. They had won the battle.

"What the..." Faith gaped at them.

But I didn't have time to explain.

The demons had realized I was good, not evil, and were heading towards me with a dangerous look.

I slipped the Cursed key out of my pocket carefully with the handkerchief.

But doing so made my safely stashed map fall from my magic pocket.

I bent down to catch the map and tucked it back in my pocket.

By then Faith had picked up the key, clueless about its power, and suddenly jolted on the spot.

"NOO!"

We screeched.

I swiftly kicked the key from her hand and stepped on the key with my trusty red boots.

Crack!

The key broke in half.

The demons faded with a hiss.

"OH!" Faith stumbled backward and shook her head in confusion.

"Just as I thought," I explained to my friends. "the demons' power came from the key, and when the key breaks, they disappear."

Looking around at all the destruction the demons had caused, I realized I would not want to face the demons in battle.

There was a shriek and a shard metal hit me in the back. I turned to see the two pirates fighting against the bars of their cage.

Well, one.

Gold was pounding on the metal while Bronze lay on the ground… sleeping?

"I will have my revenge! Come back into the caves again, and you might not be as so lucky to live!"

Gold hissed at us.

"Oh, we won't be coming back any time soon, I can promise that." I smiled. "You probably won't be doing anything until you get out of that cage."

Gold ignored me and started kicking Bronze. "Get up, you lousy first mate for nothing! Get up!"

Bronze moaned in answer, lying on the ground like a dead fish.

It was then I noticed a dark mark on each of the pirate's wings.

The mark of the cursed.

Meanwhile, the Shadow monsters looked hollow and frail, too weak to move.

They lay on the grounds, and I winced, looking away.

I jumped onto Faith in another big hug.

"Oh, Faith! I thought we were going to lose you!" We all hugged, and slowly stepped back.

"What happened, guys?" Faith asked us. "How did you get out of the dungeon? Those black stuff were demons? The stuff that attacked the shadow monsters? Are you okay?"

"Well, Pia did this weird thing-" Olivia started.

We all talked quickly at the same time as Faith fingered her bauble necklace.

"Okay, Okay," Faith hushed us. "One at a time, please."

I went first. "Faith! I just realized Lydia - the mermaid nymph we found earlier - we have to save her!"

"Yeah!" The others agreed. "Use the key but be careful."

I picked up the key warily. It was broken, so was the spell on it broken, too?

"Looking for this, fairy?" Gold sneered, dangling a key in her hand. "You want it? Let us out!"

"That's not the right key." I swam over in disbelief. "This is." I held the cursed key. "You're trying to trick me."

"That? No!" Gold chuckled. "Didn't you see the snake symbol on the key? The snake is curved like an 'S', which stands for Slate, not 'Save some random nymph in a cell'!"

"THIS?" I gasped. "This is Slate's key? But how?"

Then I remembered earlier the evil voice had said something about joining Slate, and I had denied the offer.

Gold nodded convincingly. "So free us, and you'll have the key!"

Bronze moaned, and Gold kicked her.

"No way!" I frowned, and in a swift movement, I reached out and snatched the other key from Gold's hands.

"Sorry, but we're not releasing you, Goldy-in-moldy-locks!"

"HEY!" Gold took out her pistol, but she was out of bullets. "It's GOLD, NOT whatever you just said!" she growled after us. "Also, these bars aren't moldy!"

I held Faith's hand and we swam to Lydia's cage, Faith stuttering along the way.

"What in the name of Friendship are we doing again?" Faith exclaimed, looking around at the tunnel we entered. "Can't we just leave? Like NOW?"

We didn't answer until we got to Lydia.

"Oh, I'm so glad you came back!" Lydia smiled, then looked at me. "Is she still..."

I knew she meant to say "evil", and I felt myself convulse at the remark.

Olivia and Lily filled them in while I fingered the key I had took from Gold.

"Pia…" Lily asked. "Are you okay?"

"Yeah, don't worry," I explained. "I'll get Lydia free in a matter of wing beats!"

"Careful with Slate's key." Warned Olivia.

"If I hear you cackling secretly to yourself, I'm kicking the key out of your grasp." Lily declared.

"What spell?" asked Lydia. "What are you talking about?"

Olivia and Lily explained to Lydia how the key was cursed.

I stuffed both keys, one by one, into the cell padlock.

Gold was right, the Cursed key with the 'S' on it didn't work.

When I tried the other key, the door to the cell swung open, and Lydia struggled over to me.

The weight of the chains strapped her to the ground.

I quickly freed her from her chains with the same key, then threw both keys away.

"Thank you!" Lydia swam up, twisting and turning like a baby fairy learning to fly.

She stretched and yawned as if waking up from a long, hundred-year sleep. "Thank you so much!"

"No problem." I grinned sheepishly.

My friends echoed after me, as the mermaid shook hands with each of us. Her grip was firm and her hand was warm.

Lydia smiled joyfully. "I have told you that I am a nymph. I have wings, too! OW!"

Then her pale skirt ruffled, and from it rose a set of wings with pale turquoise edges!

Her skirt was not a skirt at all; it was her folded down wings!

They were not our fairy size wings, but I could see from how they were so flexible that they could be as good as my wings.

"Are you okay?" I asked worriedly. "You said 'OW!'."

"I'm fine, it's just that I haven't stretched my wings in a long time," Lydia assured me. "To other sea creatures, that sounds weird out of my mouth!"

"Thank you for freeing me. Can I do you a favor?" Lydia asked, her eyes sweeping over us.

"OH NO!" Faith cried, seeming to remember something suddenly.

"I need to find my Friendship stone soon before sunset! Or else-" Faith gulped.

"Maui is on the brink of disaster!"

Chapter 13

THE ONE SHOWS THE WAY

After freeing Lydia, the Nymph and Guardian of the Coral Maze from her dungeon cell, I was comforting Faith.

Faith was freaked out.

"Oh no! It's almost Sunset!" she wailed. "The time to find my Friendship stone is almost over!"

Faith was getting more agitated by the second!

"We can do it! I know that we have the grit and stamina to do this!" I insisted, though I was about to collapse in worry and stress. "Let's ask Lydia, maybe she might be able to point the way. Look at your Friendship clue!"

"What if she can't help us?" Faith moaned.

Olivia finished explaining our mission to Lydia and started to comfort Faith.

"Actually, I think I might be able to help." Lydia's voice surprised us as she suddenly whisked in front of me.

"That would be really great!" I pulled Faith out from her meltdown.

She calmed down after a few minutes, then pulled out her clue from her Wing-on.

We reread the clue.

"ARR!" echoes through the dark cave,
 The one ____ ____ shows the way,
_____ ___he snake of lies and mystery,
 Cross the path of the twisted _____,
 Retrieve your stone oh so true.

"Do you know anything twisted?" I asked Lydia and showed the clue to her.

Lydia's eagle eye sped through it.

"My Coral Maze. I'm Guardian of the Coral Maze, and the coral is twisted." Lydia hesitated.

"No one has made it to the center, that was the reason I was captured by the pirates. The pirates believed there was treasure at the center of the maze and needed me to help them find it. Maybe the treasure could be your Friendship stone?"

"So, the Coral Maze should be it…" I turned to Faith. "Do you think the Coral Maze is where you will find your stone?"

"I'm not sure. But there's another line before the twisted part." Faith reminded me.

"The line notes 'he snake of lies and mystery', but there are a million sea snakes in the ocean." I explained.

"We don't know which one is the right one. 'Cross the path of the twisted' part in the clue might give us a setting as to where we are going. Then we will find the snake in that certain location."

"I guess so, but your bizarre logic is killing my brain." Faith looked thoughtfully at me, then turned to Lydia. "Say, is your Coral Maze close?"

Lydia nodded. "Once we exit this pirate hideout, we have to swim for a short while, dodge around an underwater hill, and we'll arrive at the Coral Maze."

"Give me a second to think." Faith bit her lip and fidgeted impatiently.

"We don't have a second. We should get out of here first." I stepped back from a revolting fish bone.

"Do you know the way out?" Lily asked Lydia curiously.

"It's easy, for my bond to my Coral Maze leads the way," Lydia said. "And I also feel…."

Lydia frowned.

"Much pain. Like stubbing a fin on a sharp rock, or in your saying, stubbing a toe." She looked at my boots.

"I have never seen a toe before. I thought there were five segments, not one. And why is yours red?"

"That's a boot," I told Lydia. "I'll show you what a toe looks like."

I took off my boot and wiggled my toes.

Lydia gaped at them. "That looks strange! You can actually WALK with those things? How weird! Like hands, my nymph tail fins can do this."

Lydia showed us, curling her tail fin in an attempt to pick up a piece of seaweed on the ground.

She winced, stiffly uncurling them. "My fins have been aching lately. I wonder why. Maybe I'm out of practice picking up seaweed."

"Maybe because it's too cold here, it's freezing me into a popsicle!" Lily joked.

Lydia cocked her head. "What's a popsicle?"

"A frozen treat, I'll go into details later."

"Like iced cream? Or sorbet?"

"Sort of." I told her as I was hit by realization.

I placed a hand on Faith's shoulders.

"I figured out the second line of the clue! The one who's caged shows the way!"

"The smudged part should be 'who's caged'!" We exclaimed together.

As I said, that, Faith gasped and looked at the clue.

"Seems like you're right Pia!" she yipped.

The second line was no longer smudged.

"ARR!" echoes through the dark cave,
The one who's caged shows the way,
_____ ___he snake of lies and mystery,
Cross the path of the twisted Coral,
Retrieve your stone oh so true.

"Now, let's go!" We swam around the tunnels and after what seemed like forever, I saw an opening.

The others had seen it too, as for it gave us a burst of energy.

Lydia snorted with amusement as Olivia and Lily shot towards the exit hole like a pod of wild dolphins.

I gripped Faith's hand tighter as I tugged her, catching up with the others.

I suddenly felt a strong current as Lydia picked up speed and passed us.

With a strong tail like hers, and nymph wings to help, she was up ahead.

But she slowed down unexpectedly, like losing energy.

I guessed it was to give us a chance to catch up.

I looked at Faith and taking her hand, I swam faster.

I heard a suppressed wail of pain and saw her stub her fin on a rock. She looked at me and nodded.

She was okay.

We swam faster and faster, and light blinded us all.

I reached out aimlessly and felt a shaking hand pulling me forward.

"We're out!" Lydia breathed, swimming forward. She looked around at the bare ocean ground and wailed.

"But where are all the sea creatures?" Olivia gasped in horror. "I don't see a single living plant in sight!"

"What happened here?" I asked Lydia. "Where is all the life?"

Lydia shook her head, distressed.

146

"I don't know. The land around the Coral Maze has always been full of life. The Coral Maze is loved by the creatures that live in it, and the creatures depend on the Coral Maze to bring life to the plants for food and shelter."

Lydia stopped swimming and shook her head.

"It looks as if all the animals have moved away!" Lydia swam down, scooping up a handful of soil. "The soil is no longer fertile for plants to grow here!"

"OH NO!" Lily cried.

Lydia whipped around. "That must mean…"

Lydia looked gravely at me, panic sparking as she waved her tail.

"Something has happened to my Coral Maze!"

She took off in a rush and we followed. "I have to see my Coral Maze! It should be right behind that hill!"

Lydia shot towards the hill, and at the last second, swerved to the side.

"Wait up!" I called and Lydia took my hand, pulling me forward.

Faith, Olivia, and Lily held each other's hands as Lydia propelled us forward.

It seemed like we were swimming forever around the underwater hill, when Lydia gasped.

In front of us stood Lydia's Coral Maze.

It was as if the color pigments of the red Coral Maze had been washed away by a coming tide of darkness.

The Coral Maze was as ghastly as a graveyard.

I felt a cold wave of dread overcome me.

The Coral Maze was not what I imagined at all.

Chapter 14

THE FALL OF THE CORAL

"What?" Faith breathed.

Our newfound friend Lydia gasped in horror, staring at her Coral Maze she was to protect.

"What has happened to my home?" she swam down to the coral, her tail tip brushing the dusty ground.

The Coral Maze was not much at all.

The rows of once proud coral had slumped in defeat, and the red color was rusted and frayed.

One poke at the coral might send it toppling down for it was infested with algae.

But even the green slimy algae were broken down too. It had no nutrients, nothing to live on after sucking power from the coral.

It just sat on the Coral Maze, weighing it down, its only use was as waste.

Surrounding the Coral Maze, was a circle of coral. Olivia perched on the top of it carefully.

And next to that, lay many rotting remains of what I perceived The Breath of the Sea flower!

The once probably powerful looking tiki pole had lost the gleam in its eyes, replaced with defeat.

"That's an ancient tiki statue of Kane, the god of light and life." Faith whispered to me, pointing at the tiki pole.

I nodded in fascination but looked in pity at the crying Lydia.

Tears streamed down Lydia's cheeks.

"The ancient tiki poles can't help me protect the Coral Maze anymore from the darkness of evil. This is why every day my magic weakens more, and every second is filled with agitating pain." Lydia wailed.

"The darkness has spread far, and with no Friendship to stop it, with

Friendship dying, my Coral Maze dies with it."

Silence filled the once paradise.

Lydia bowed her head to the Coral Maze.

Faith, Olivia, Lily and I respectfully bowed too.

Lydia pressed the palm of her hand to the coral, and I could feel sorrow welling up inside her.

Instantly, like she was hit with electricity, Lydia trembled silently.

Then she collapsed onto the dusty sea ground.

"Lydia!" Faith, Olivia, Lily and I cried in unison, rushing to her side.

Lydia's eyes were glazed over with fever, and her wings had suddenly lost their lively color. Her nymph scales were darkened and dull.

"I feel their pain." Lydia whispered. "Their sorrow, grief, distress. I wasn't here when the Coral Maze started dying. I didn't have the chance to try to save it."

"W-what can we do to help you?" I pressed her urgently.

"Me? Nothing." Lydia struggled to sit up, but she was paralyzed like the coral, unable to do anything.

"Find your Friendship stone. Defeat Slate of Chaos. Save Friendship and Maui before death comes for all.

"Then my Coral Maze will thrive again and happiness will fill the gap that was opened."

Faith was silent.

"Now we must take you somewhere safe." Olivia proclaimed, and lifted Lydia's tail silently.

My friends held onto Lydia, and we swam towards a tall clump of seagrass and set her down.

"Here. No one will find you. You'll be safe here." I grabbed a few pieces of kelp and set it over Lydia like a blanket.

"Thank you." She whispered.

"To find your stone, go into the Coral Maze. A prize lies inside the maze, but none know what prize lies inside."

Lydia leaned close to me.

"Remember this above all others. Follow your heart and fill it with stamina and grit."

I nodded vigorously.

Lydia sighed softly with a voice full of pain as she drowsily turned her head slowly to look better at us.

Then there was a soft sigh, and Lydia was asleep.

"Thank you for helping us." I thanked her solemnly.

We left her side slowly.

Lily glanced back, trembling.

The Coral Maze, Lydia's life, the future of Maui, and friendship were all on our shoulders!

We swam towards the Coral Maze, wondering if it was our destiny to venture inside.

"The other line in my clue..." Faith trailed off, and I knew what she was thinking.

"Maybe we encounter it in the maze," I suggested.

"But it's before the twisted part." Faith said. "And we don't know if this maze is part of the clue. It has twisted coral, but many other things can be twisted too! And all the animals here have already moved away, and maybe that snake moved away too!"

Silence.

Faith gulped and swam forward.

"We'll have to trust the Coral Maze." I followed her down the path, the others close behind.

The dusty coral loomed over us as we swam by.

We huddled closer to each other, linking arms. The usual stubbornly brave Olivia shuddered, looking at the dying, weak coral.

A wave of water slammed into my face as a dark blue-grey tail flashed into view.

"What was that?"

Some creature weaved in between us, water flurrying in its wake.

"Who are you? Show yourself!"

Faith demanded, but her voice was more question then challenge.

I backed up, squeaking when I hit Lily.

The whirling creature slowed, and we saw it was none other than an eel!

A Moray eel.

Its fangs were bared, and its tongue lolled in its mouth.

"HALT!" The eel hissed, and a fresh wave of electricity flowed down its spine.

Then it controlled itself and forced the excess energy to stay in its body.

"You may not go any further, strangers! In the maze lies a great prize, only those worthy enough shall take it!"

"We are coming for a good cause," I told it. "Please, might you let us pass?"

The eel blinked, then opened its mouth.

If you believe it so,
if you want to cross,
first you must pass a test.
Troubling thought and danger lie ahead.
The coral around you all looks the same.
What should you do,
should have thought twice.
You can't go back.

The eel finished the song with a click of its tongue as it stared at us once more. "Do you still want to pass me?"

"Yes." Faith nodded eagerly. "Please, Ms. eel!"

"Are you sure?" the eel countered, weaving in between each fairy and inspecting us closely.

"Once you decide, you cannot go back. Think carefully, now."

"We want to pass!" Faith, Olivia, Lily and I chorused together.

"We aren't afraid!" Lily exclaimed bravely, biting her lip. "Sort of!"

"Very well. I'm guessing you'll change your mind once your challenge has begun. None have enough stamina and grit to find the center of the maze. Good luck."

The eel turned its back on us and rolled its eyes as it muttered something about stubborn younglings and idiotic children.

It swam forward and turned into another corner and out of sight.

"Wait up!" I followed it. The others formed a single file line behind me.

Suddenly I halted, and we all collided with each other.

"OW!" Olivia cried, rubbing her cheek. "Why did you stop?"

"Sorry!" I grunted, trying to swim forward. My arms waved. "I'm stuck! And trying to swim forward! But I'm not moving!"

"You're what?" Faith cried.

"But you're just clawing at the water. There's nothing there to hold you back!" she stared in disbelief at me.

I took a step back and made a swimming start at the invisible water wall.

"Ug!" I kicked the water and felt a hard wall.

Faith poked at the water in front of her a few times, then shook her head. "Nothing."

"You're poking at the wrong spot!"

"Oops! He-he!"

We experimented a few more times.

"Is this a wall?" Olivia asked curiously, tapping her toe on the ground. "Or are we going crazy? Or is it the first challenge?"

I didn't have time to register what Olivia had just said as a sudden current gusted into the invisible wall and exploded.

Green algae swam into the water and blocked our vision like a dust cloud. I gasped as a drowsy feeling came over me and I drowsily looked around.

"Greetings, flies." Drawled a cold voice, frightening me.

I looked around into the green algae but spotted nothing.

Suddenly the green was cleared by a gloved hand.

I found in front of me, the horrible, evil Slate of Chaos!

Chapter 15
WHOM TO SACRIFICE?

Slate of Chaos, the opposite of friendship, the chaos stirrer, and the cruelest wingless fairy in history, was standing in front of me.

I barely recognized him.

My friends had described to me how Slate looked the last time he had dared to show his face.

But he had changed very much.

He wore a full-body black suit, with white gloves and boots. He also had a white belt which had a key sign in the middle.

His face was crested with fancy armor-like stuff.

The only things that hadn't changed were his yellow piercing eyes that could blow a large hole in the biggest of mountains.

And wherever Slate went, you would instantly start shivering.

Clouds shrouded his body as he moved freely around me.

A shiver went down my spine, even at just looking at him.

I stepped backward, whining silently, and bumped into something solid.

"AGH!" I jumped up, then turned around and gasped.

My friends Faith, Olivia, and Lily were sitting behind me.

I spotted a rope tied tightly around them. Their screaming was muffled by gags.

Giant spiders loomed over them, as if guarding them from me.

"Faith! Olivia! Lily!" I screamed, ignoring the giant spiders.

I bent down and tried to untie the rope binding them.

Slate smirked.

The giant spiders just stared blankly ahead.

I desperately tried to unbind my friends, but they kept fidgeting as if they didn't hear me.

"Faith!" I cried. "Olivia! Lily!"

None of my friends seemed to hear me.

They were staring aimlessly as I tried to get their attention.

Slate twirled an object on his finger and cackled madly.

"Look, I've got all three Friendship stones!" he held out his hands and showed me the Friendship stones.

"What happens if I destroy them, hmm?"

"NOOO!" I screeched, and lunged at him, hands out.

Slate dodged with ease and I collided into the dirt, coughing hard.

"HEY FAIRY!" Slate slid his fingernails into the earth and opened a crack.

Lava flowed freely underneath.

And as Slate stomped on the ground, more cracks appeared, spreading towards my struggling, bound friends.

"FAITH! OLIVIA! LILY!" I wailed, starting towards them as the earth split wider and threatened to swallow them whole.

Lava sprouted up in furious fountains, scattering droplets everywhere.

The giant spiders turned and vanished.

I gripped Faith's hand and pulled Faith, Olivia, and Lily up.

They were too heavy.

"Hey, fairy!" Slate crowed at me. "Having fun?" he set the three Friendship stones down a distance across from my friends.

Then he dug his nails into the ground once more.

The earth rumbled beneath my feet, knocking me away from my friends.

Cracks appeared, and the earth split as lava flowed underneath both my friends and the Friendship stones.

I gasped as I realized what he was doing.

Clever Slate.

He had set down the Friendship stones very far to my right, and my friends very far to the left.

And I was in the middle of them.

"How do you like when your most precious thing disappears?" Slate cackled like a mad fairy possessed.

His eyeballs were swirling dangerously in his head.

I was almost afraid his eyeballs would pop out and chase me forever across the world.

"Choose! The Friendship stones, or your three friends!" Slate shrieked.

"Will you choose the three Friendship stones?" he gestured to my right.

The Friendship stones were sitting helplessly as the lava neared.

"Or will you choose your friends?" Slate pointed to my left, where my friends seemed to be unconscious of what was happening.

"They're too far apart. You can only get to one in time before the lava swallows them!"

"YOU can't do this!" I tearfully protested, but I knew the answer.

"Oh, no. I just did." Slate snickered.

Lava swirled beneath Faith, Olivia, and Lily, waiting impatiently for its next meal.

I gasped, trying to catch my breath.

I wildly looked between the Friendship stones and my friends, the Friendship fairies.

Friendship stones and my friends lay on my shaking shoulders.

What did Slate mean?

I couldn't choose between saving the Friendship stones and my friends.

I cherished them all!

But Slate was right.

There wasn't enough time to get to both Friendship stone and fairies.

So which one would I chose? Both were extremely precious and important to me and Maui.

My friends were wedged between the two split sides of the earth.

The lava underneath them was rising higher and higher rapidly, threatening to swallow them.

"You can't do this, Slate! You can't!" I sobbed helplessly.

"I just did!" Slate watched me through yellow eyes. "You don't have time to save both, fairy!"

"Choose your friends and you've doomed Maui!"

"Choose the Friendship stones, and your friends die!"

The lava was less than a wingspan away from both the Friendship stones and my friends.

"Friendship stones or your friends?" Slate boomed. "Choose NOW!"

"I...I..." I trailed off, as a dumb tear appeared in my eyes, blurring my vision.

"I choose..."

"TIME UP!" Slate screeched.

"TIME FOR YOUR FRIENDS AND THE FRIENDSHIP STONES TO MEET THEIR DOOM!"

My hair got into my mouth and stung my eyes.

My tears were streaming down my cheeks like a river down a mountain.

I could only watch as my friends were about to meet their doom.

I was too late.

I had failed them.

I had failed Maui.

"NOOOOOOOOO!"

Chapter 16
THE CHALLENGE

"Pia!" one voice called.

"Pia! Are you okay?" that voice - it couldn't be - could it?

Faith?

"Ignore her!" Slate screeched at me.

"Your friends are dead, dead!"

"They were swallowed by the lava! There is no one here for you! I repeat, no one!"

Confidence had escaped his voice.

What replaced it was fear and uncertainty.

"Darkness will flood Maui! The Friendship stones have dissolved, and every fairy and creature will bow down to me!" Slate yowled.

I looked around.

The cracks of lava who had swallowed up my friends were gone.

But then, who was calling me?

Clouds of dark purple swirled around me, blocking my vision.

I gasped. One of the clouds looked like Slate's new commander, Crusher.

In fact, all the clouds appeared to be in a spider shape!

The ground was made up of black kelp now, the earth and dust had vanished from view.

I reached out a hand and waved it around.

Slate started towards me. "No! Not there, silly fairy! There's nothing there!"

I didn't give any hint that I had heard him, but instead, I continued to wave my hands around, walking into the mist.

I struck the ground but no lava appeared, even as I tried to wedge open a crack. "I know your trick."

"This is all an illusion!" I turned to Slate of Chaos.

"You liar! Friendship shall be restored and darkness will never reign over the good creatures of Maui!"

Slate stumbled back and I walked forward, facing him with confidence.

"We will save Friendship, no matter what!"

Cold water blew past my ears as I faced Slate.

He was blurring before my very eyes.

"NO! NO! NOOO!" Slate shrieked.

Within a heartbeat, Slate was gone.

I gasped, sitting up with a start.

Faith was crouched over me, glancing at me worriedly. "How are you?" Faith asked me.

"Fine." I groaned. "Other than scared out of my skin, I'm totally fine." Faith informed me what happened to her, and I told her about my illusion.

"Wait!" I cried. "Faith, show me your clue."

Faith pulled it from her Wing-on.

"The clue is supposed to say, '*Meet t*' in the smudged part!" I nodded confidently.

"You're right. Look!" Faith gasped.

The clue now said:

"ARR!" echoes through the dark cave,
The one who's caged shows the way,
Meet the snake of lies and mystery,
Cross the path of the twisted _____,
Retrieve your stone oh so true.

Olivia and Lily were lying on the ground beside me and had started to stir, mumbling and crying out loud.

"Let's wake them up," I said, crouching down next to Olivia.

We soon woke them up.

Olivia and Lily both wore faces full of sweat and whimpered before realizing where they were.

"Be brave." Faith whispered over and over again. "Be brave, fight your fears."

"Easy for you to say." Olivia panted out of earshot. "You don't know what I went through!"

Lily was trembling next to her and exclaimed, "It was horrible!"

We filled them in on the clue, and they cheered.

"Now where's that eel?" I wondered.

Faith took the lead, swimming around.

She screeched in shock as the eel turned the corner.

"Well done." The eel glanced at us, a grin on her face. "You passed this one. Your next challenges will all be real. It requires quick thinking and courage, though it is not mine to give."

The eel mischievously opened her jaw and continued in an important tone of voice.

"It is your journey to find the Friendship stones."

"If you make it out of the Coral Maze alive, and with your prize, I just might congratulate you. But be forewarned, you may come in but you might not come out."

The eel continued with a glint in her eyes. "And also, whatever you do, don't venture into the left path. That is, if you don't want a horrible death!"

"Okay…" Olivia murmured to Lily. "'Well done!', she says! Left path. A horrible death! Hmm…"

"Wait! How do you know about the Friendship stones???"

The eel gave us a short nod, then disappeared out of sight, weary with sleep.

Olivia glanced at the path to the left and stepped forward, looking around. "There aren't any monsters here, are there? What did that eel mean by 'horrible death?'"

"Wait, Olivia!" Lily yelped. "Watch out for that-"

Olivia's leg got caught in a tangle of seaweed that lifted her upside down.

"EEEEK!" Olivia screamed, thrashing in the water, and aimed a water bubble at the seaweed.

"Get off me!" There was a clunk as Olivia was dropped back to the ground.

The eel's snickering face appeared around the corner. "Gotcha! HA! HA! Tricked ya! Trick or treat, you choose the trick! HA!"

"It's not Halloween yet!" Olivia got to her feet. "And did you really have a treat?"

And being the smart one, the eel quickly disappeared with a flick of her tail.

The seaweed let out a cloud of dust that engulfed Olivia as she tried to get on her feet.

It made her cough loudly.

"What is this plant?" Olivia muttered.

She reached out and touched the seaweed before pulling out a small pouch with a bit of dust on the edges.

"So when I walked in, this plant tangled on my leg because of that thing-a-ma-bob, and that compressed the end of this that squirted that dust onto me!" Olivia exclaimed, examining the prank trap with great awe.

"This is a good trap for an eel who all she probably has is seaweed, kelp, and disgusting dust!"

Faith wasn't listening.

"Over here!" Faith said suddenly, taking off to the path on the right.

We followed in a hurry, Olivia grumbling all the while.

Chapter 17
SOUR SNAKES

We swam around in the Coral Maze for a while, but Faith was getting agitated and Olivia kept itching her arm.

"I was sprayed with itching dust!" Olivia groaned, scratching her head. "I'm so itchy!"

Lily kept adding more paste to the parts where Olivia had been powdered with itch dust.

Meanwhile Faith swam everywhere in a rush, and in a loop-de-loop too out of anxiety and nervousness.

I let her take the lead, and I hung back with the others.

Olivia was telling Lily about the time before she found her Friendship talent.

She finished just as I joined them and greeted me with a friendly hi. Lily nodded her head, and I suspected she hadn't listened at all to Olivia's story.

"You know, it's as if the eel can predict the future!" Olivia rubbed her arm.

"I was tied up with Faith and Lily while Slate tried to destroy the Friendship stones. Then my dream switched. I was hanging upside down, suspended by a vine. I was then sprayed with itching dust, and I couldn't stop scratching my arm! It was awful! And realistic! Want to hear the full story?"

"I'll pass this time."

"Ok. I wonder why that eel is still here." Olivia thoughtfully murmured, echoing my thoughts. "All the other animals have moved away."

"There are no living plants around here." Lily looked at the algae resting on the coral. "I think a certain animal will enjoy eating that algae."

"The algae probably only grew because there were no more animals to eat the algae off the Coral Maze." I considered everything that had happened.

Lily nodded in agreement.

"PIA! OLIVIA! LILY!" Came a yell. "It's Faith. Um, I'm lost."

I looked around. Faith was gone.

"Faith! We're over here!" I replied as loud as I could while trying to stay calm. Faith had wandered deeper into the Coral Maze.

I hoped she hadn't gone too far.

Our chances were slim of finding her in this one big maze. "Stay where you are, we'll try to find you!"

We quickened our paces, looking around in every corner and shadow.

I approached the edge of another path and spotted a snake-like figure moving in the shadow. "Eel?" I uncertainly asked.

Silence. I peered closer, squinting my eyes as I looked into the shadow.

"BOO!" A jaw of a moray eel shot forward into my face.

"YOW!" I screamed, jumping backward. I recovered quickly and realized the Eel was treading right in front of me.

"Oh! You." I narrowed my eyes. "Please, I don't want to be pranked!"

The eel rolled its eyes. "As if I would do such a thing, create trouble." It smirked. "Call the other fairies over here if you want my help to find your lost friend, peewee."

"Hey! I'm not a peewee! Look at yourself! If I'm a peewee, you're an ant!" I retorted indignantly.

The eel blinked. "What's an ant?"

"Nothing, just a land animal. You wouldn't know of it." I muttered. "Fine, I'll call my friends."

When Olivia and Lily returned from searching, the eel continued. "Your friend - the brat - got lost searching for her stupid stone. I can find her."

Olivia intervened, glaring at the eel suspiciously. "How can we trust you? You're really sour for a snake! And mean! You already pranked me with itching dust! And you're a complete stranger!"

"You're too trusting of strangers in the first place! I don't know if it's in your nature, or you're actually that dumb."

Olivia steamed, and I could see fire burning in her eyes. "I'm not dumb! Don't call me that!"

"Whaaat – ever! But anyway, what other solution can you think of?" the eel retorted and started forward.

I swam up to look over the Coral, but the Coral Maze had an invisible ceiling that prevented me from going through to find Faith.

I tried a few more times in an attempt to break through the ceiling but ended up with a big bruise on my head.

"Great." I moaned and descended. "Just great."

"You'll have to trust me!" the eel grinned and swam back down. "Don't try too many times at that, it's no use. The Coral Maze still retains some magic! There is a magical ceiling, by the way!"

Olivia stuck her tongue out when the eel wasn't looking, then hid it, remembering she was a Friendship fairy.

The eel swam up.

She was far past the magical ceiling, glancing around in search of Faith.

"How can you swim up?" I inquired. "Is this a trick?"

"NO!" scoffed the eel, looking proud. "I'm VIP! I'm part of the maze, one with the maze, I'm SPECIAL!"

"Oh. Cool. Stay where you are, Faith!" I yelled, cupping my hands over my mouth to make my voice heard.

"Don't wander! Eel is helping us find you!"

We followed the eel as it confidently exclaimed, "She's close!" every few minutes.

"We don't have much time to find the Friendship stones!" Olivia complained to the eel after the eel had exclaimed, "She's close!" for like the seventh time. Or maybe the eighth time.

"Can you hurry in your search? We're in a hurry, for goodness sake, and we need to get a move on!"

"She's close!" grunted the eel.

"Well, we're stressed!" Olivia retorted. "Can you even find Faith or not?"

"Of course, I can!" the eel muttered under its breath. "Have some stamina, will you?"

I jolted, remembering Lydia had mentioned the word "stamina" earlier.

"Faith! Stay right where you are and don't wander any further!" Olivia called out, deciding to ignore the eel.

"But my Friendship stone! It's here somewhere!" came the frantic reply. "I-I need to find it! Oh, where are you my beloved stone?"

Faith's voice echoed off different paths of the Coral Maze.

"Fluttering fairies!" I sighed. "She's probably flying er, swimming around now."

"This way." The eel butted into our conversation. "And hurry! She's swimming everywhere, but she's close. Just like my wild grandbabies…"

"I was like this when I felt my Friendship stone," Lily whispered to me while swimming. "I don't blame Faith. It must be close. Even I can feel it!"

I nodded in acknowledgment and swam quickly in a flurry of bubbles behind the eel.

The others followed.

"Ever since I was chosen by the Friendship stone, my world changed." Lily told me.

She stopped herself from rolling her eyes as the eel shouted out that Faith was close once more. "I was honored that the Friendship stones chose me. But at the same time, it was such a big responsibility!"

I nodded, then thought about the Friendship stones. Without it, time was ticking before destruction.

And even I and the other gentle Friendship fairies were getting frustrated!

"Here!" the eel flicked its tail to a Coral wall dead end where Faith was rambling to herself.

Faith quickly spotted us.

"PIA! OLIVIA! LILY!" Faith sprang onto us, giving us a quick hug. "Oh, my Friendship stone, it's here somewhere, I can feel it, but it's so confusing - the power is emitting from - everywhere! We have to hurry, someone might have taken it, I was so lost…"

Faith blurted out in a rush.

"Just a second." I hesitated. "We have to thank the -"

"We don't have a second!" Faith interrupted me. "Oh, Pia, I'll never forgive myself if Slate destroys Friendship! What would I do?"

Faith suddenly seemed to forget we were there as she jolted up.

"It's here somewhere. I feel your presence, my stone, please reveal yourself! Are you over here? Where did you go? I thought you were there a second ago, but you disappeared!"

She swam around and checked every corner and left no pebble unturned.

I thanked the eel and it gracefully slithered away, looking smug.

Turning back to my friends, I saw that Faith and Olivia had disappeared and Lily was looking around wildly.

"Pia!" She rushed over and tugged me to the spot Faith was last. "When you were talking to the eel, Faith wandered and Olivia followed." Lily announced.

"I stayed behind to fetch you but lost the others. I only know they went into the middle path! What should we do?"

"Hold my hand," I told her, swimming into the middle passageway.

I strained my ear.

Yells came from my right. I turned right and listened again.

The noise sounded closer this time.

Lily saw what I was doing and quickly caught on.

We turned a few more corners and looked around. Olivia's head popped up from one corner as she spotted me.

"Pia!" she cried, panting for breath. "Faith-" she grunted. "Help me get her-" she gasped. "UGH!"

We were already by her side, helping her drag Faith back.

We sat Faith down and I reviewed what we knew about the Coral Maze. "Alright. Lydia told us about how the animals used to live here - sort of."

"Yeah," Olivia added. "And she also said something about the damage to the peace and harmony in her home."

"And I know my map won't work here. We have to try something else." I held up my tattered map.

My map showed our location, and a big round red circle that represented the Coral Maze.

It did not show the passages or which path would lead to the center of the Coral Maze, but that was my map being mysterious.

"There was also something else Lydia said… her last words to us before we entered the maze." I said thoughtfully.

"She said that to find the Friendship stone, we would make it to the center of the maze."

I looked at Faith, whose eyes were darting around to possible paths to her stone.

"Try to focus and think about your Friendship stone. Close your eyes a bit and that might help." I suggested.

Faith shook her head and stood up.

Olivia tensed. Then Faith sighed and slowly sat down.

"Okay, Pia. I'll try." She shut her eyes tight and she bit her lip. Her arms reached out and pointed to different paths, tingling slightly.

"Relax, Faith. Relax." I soothed her, but she didn't move. I got worried.

What would happen to Friendship?

I was sure it was almost sunset.

Olivia's belly rumbled in hunger, and she blushed, embarrassed.

"Don't worry. We only had one meal the whole day. It's okay to be hungry." Lily assured her, distributing sour snake candies.

I picked up a blue raspberry Sour Snake from her large packet.

Blue raspberry sour snakes were my FAVORITE!

I loved it because it was so tangy and sour. And I loved sour candies. Especially blue ones.

The Sour Snake I held wriggled from my grasp and hissed, swimming toward Faith.

I quickly caught it and bit off its tail. The sour snake turned immobile.

"The first time I had these, I was scared of the snakes." Olivia smiled ruefully, munching ravenously on three green apple snakes. "The snakes were hissing really loudly, and I flew up onto the counter and wouldn't get off. My parents had to use a wrench to pry me off."

She paused for laughter but found none. I was still chewing and Lily was reaching for a red cherry Sour Snake.

She dropped the packet by accident and all the sour snakes escaped, swimming around wildly.

Eel popped around a corner and greedily gobbled the snakes down before Lily had the chance to stand up.

"Hey!" Lily glared an Eel, who only sheepishly shrugged.

"Out here with nothing to eat, you must be hungry." softening, Lily tossed Eel another sour snake and turned back to listen to Olivia's story.

"Later I found out sour snakes were enchanted and that they weren't real snakes. They turn immobile after you bite them." Olivia finished.

I chewed thoughtfully on the snake's tail.

"I have a similar story," Lily added in and begun her story.

I turned to check on Faith.

Faith was holding her breath nervously, and I could tell so because she was ominously still.

I prodded her with a finger, and she exhaled in surprise, like a balloon letting out air.

"I-I can't! W-w-we have to get going. I cannot stop. This won't work!" Faith opened her eyes. "I have to find my Friendship stone."

Olivia jolted upwards, accidentally knocking Lily over. I braced myself to pursue Faith in case she swam off to find her stone again.

Faith stood there, standing like a statue.

I met Faith's gaze and she sat down.

Faith sighed, face full of frustration.

Olivia relaxed, though she looked wary, gulping down the last of the green apple sour snakes.

Lily looked at Faith intently, as if doing so would make everything alright again and the Friendship in Maui restored and the terrible Slate of Chaos defeated.

I recognized this as hope, a spark as Faith had described, and one more thing.

One thing that was more than I could describe with words.

But trying to simplify it, I knew Lily's staring was from the heart, with longing and a desire for everything to be okay.

From the heart.

I smiled. Something had popped into my mind.

I scooted over to Faith's side and motioned for her to kneel down.

"Follow your heart." I whispered sincerely. This piece of advice was from my heart, and I wasn't thinking of Lydia's advice.

"You HAVE the stamina to find your Friendship stone."

I was giving my own advice.

"Concentrate and think. Think of your stone. Feel its presence around you and it will help to guide you. Desire to have it in your hands, as the feeling of family warmth."

A small smile formed on Faith's face.

"I have faith in you, Faith." I grinned cheekily at her. "Please, try."

"What is it?" Olivia called softly. Lily was checking the contents of her Wing-on.

I didn't reply.

Not that I didn't want to tell the others.

I just felt only Faith would know what to do and this piece of advice was just for her.

She had been so stressed out lately, she just wasn't herself anymore.

I wanted the real Faith back.

Chapter 18
THE CENTER OF THE MAZE

Faith stood up slowly with much caution, and we held hands.

"Follow your heart." She murmured slowly, as if finally understanding a new language.

"My heart lies with the stone and to the stone I go." She sang softly and swam forward a few paces.

Faith closed her eyes.

Her breathing slowed.

"No matter where, beware, I'll find my precious stone."

I gripped her hand as she led me around a corner. Olivia and Lily looked at each other before quickly following.

We turned many more corners and followed different paths, Faith singing all the while.

"To climb a mountain what a feat, I'll do some wacky stunts! To overcome evil and stop their armies! From rising!" Faith hummed.

Her eyes were still closed, though she dodged all the coral and didn't bump into anything.

It was as if she had a visual map in her mind.

"My heart lies with my stone and to the stone I go." Faith repeated the first verse of her song.

Then she led me around another corner and opened her eyes.

Out of breath, Olivia and Lily swam up from behind us.

"What-are-you-doing?" Olivia huffed. "We are completely lost! What should we do now…? "

Olivia stopped and blinked.

She rubbed her eyes.

She smacked her cheek.

She pinched her neck.

She pulled her hair, then said, "NO WAY…"

In front of us, in a circle of coral, on a silver platform, sat a rosy pink rock.

It looked partly worn away, but even age could not disguise its sparkle.

It glowed, giving me a feeling of comfort.

The Friendship stone.

I squeezed my eyes shut and opened them again.

After all the struggles and obstacles we had faced, we had finally found the Friendship stone.

I sighed, recalling today's adventures.

Everything, every second of today, I would remember and hold it close to my heart.

But it was relieving to know that we now had Faith's Friendship stone.

And with that, we would finally save Maui and stop Slate in his tracks.

The rosy pink rock was still sitting in front of me, glinting as if trying to remind me of all my memories with my precious friends.

Faith was frozen with shock and pure delight.

Olivia and Lily had fainted with glee.

I took out the picture with my friends, tracing my finger over every fairy's face.

I could see my reflection in the glossy picture looking back at me.

I felt warm and toasty.

It was like slurping up a cup of hot chocolate, safe and snug in a cottage while outside a huge blizzard raged.

I tucked the picture back into my pocket.

Faith blinked. "My Friendship stone…"

"I knew you had the stamina and grit to find the Friendship stone," I exclaimed. "We did it!"

When Faith didn't reply, I poked her. "Aren't you supposed to get your stone or do at least something?"

"Huh? Oh! Oh!" Faith stumbled forward and tripped over a clump of kelp. "Ow!"

I stepped forward to help.

She groaned and hauled herself back onto her feet, swimming to her Friendship stone.

Faith proceeded forward and slowly placed a trembling hand on her stone.

There was a flash of white and I staggered backward.

A wave of warming energy overcame me and I collapsed.

"Pia?" A nudge to the side. "Pia? Are you awake?"

"Yup. Give me a second." I stumbled to my feet, accidentally slapping Faith.

"Whoa! Sorry!" I cried, stretching my legs.

"Never mind that." Faith said brightly. "Look what I've got!' She pulled out a rosy stone.

Her Friendship stone!

"I got it while you guys decided to go to sleep!" Faith smiled.

She clenched her hand into a fist, raising the pinky and her thumb.

I copied her cluelessly.

"Shaka! This is the shaka sign." Faith explained, giving her shaka a little shake. "Don't worry, don't rush."

"Whoo-hoo!" Olivia cheered, making a shaka sign too.

I leaped in surprise, realizing they were awake, just behind me.

Lily did an underwater cartwheel.

"Shaka, everyone! Don't worry, don't rush!" Faith gushed happily.

"Slate doesn't stand a chance!"

"Because we got the Friendship stone!" We all cheered.

"Now let's go to the Friendship Point!" yelled Faith.

"What?" I asked, combing dirt from my hair. "You mean you can't just touch the Friendship stones right now to recharge Friendship?"

"It's not that simple. The Friendship Point is a special place in Maui where we Friendship fairies restore Friendship." Faith explained.

I swam up and down in a full body nod.

"Wait! I know the last part of the clue!" Olivia piped up. We turned to her expectantly.

"The last smudged blank is supposed to say 'coral'!" she proudly smiled.

"Oh, yes!" I proclaimed. "You did it! You're a genius, Olivia!"

Faith pulled the clue from her Wing-on.

We read it out loud.

"ARR!" echoes through the dark cave,
The one who's caged shows the way,
Meet the snake of lies and mystery,
Cross the path of the twisted coral,
Retrieve your stone oh so true.

"Now let's get out of the Coral Maze!" Faith swam forward, then stopped. "Pia, did you happen to remember the route we used to come in?"

I hesitated, rummaging in my pockets. I pulled out my map. "Ta-da! My magical map!"

"All right." Faith swam to my side and peered at my map closely. "Wait, didn't you say your map was blank?"

"The Coral Maze's magic is preventing it from mapping the route, to stop cheaters. But my map is special." I muttered. "It records every step I take with it."

I closed my eyes and thought of a simple spell.

"Reverse, reverse,
think back in time.
Show me the way
to head that's right."

My map sparkled, and I waited breathlessly.

On my map, four dots appeared at the start of the Coral Maze, each a different color. "That's us!" Faith cried.

My map glowed, and vivid red lines, dots, and slashes appeared, marking the Coral Maze trails.

A blue line trailed from where our dots stood, trailing to the center of the Coral Maze.

"That's us when we came in, the four dots on my map! Now, all we have to do is to use my map to follow the trail out!" I exclaimed, then furrowed my brow.

Some strange dark splotches of ink were moving towards the Coral Maze entrance.

I wondered what the splotches of ink meant.

Anyway, we had a clear path out of the Coral Maze. We could see what the black splotches were later.

"Now let's go!" I took off. "That way!"

Faith's legs moved so fast, I could swear if she didn't slow down soon, she would create a whirlpool!

Olivia and Lily sped after us in a hurry.

My map buzzed in my fingers, each buzz louder than the last as I swam faster, sparkles erupting out of my map.

The map became hot, and I quickly hit the parchment paper, afraid the map would somehow burst into flames while underwater.

Faith quickened her pace once Olivia and Lily were next to us.

"Good job!" The eel had popped out from behind a passageway. I skidded to a stop.

Olivia and Lily crashed into me.

"Thank you!" Faith and I smiled.

"Em, do you have er, a moment? In private?" The eel nervously asked.

"Yeah, give me a second." I anxiously glanced at Faith.

"Alright, we'll wait here." Faith sat down patiently, and Lily started to distribute sour snakes from her Wing-on.

"I don't want to slow you down. I'll catch up in a moment. Meet you by the Coral Maze entrance?" I grabbed Lily's notepad and her pen and jotted down my instructions.

"When you see the hunk of coral shaped like a flying hedgehog, turn left, then pass the next corridor…"

"Thanks." Faith nodded, Olivia, saluted, and Lily grinned, sucking on a purple Sour Snake.

I swam over to the eel as my friends left.

"Hey." The eel looked down. "You're leaving, and…"

"Do you want to come with us?" I asked her gently. "You're very welcome too!"

"I would love to come with you. But alas, I cannot stray from the Coral Circle." The eel hesitated. "I have a story to tell."

"About how you learned to be a master prankster?" I joked lightly, though I was disappointed she would not be coming.

"You'll learn soon enough about my curse." The eel sighed.

"Curse?" I gasped. "Wait…" the eel didn't acknowledge or hear me.

"It was a mighty nice day in the ocean. It was sunny, and this very spot was bustling of fish and sea turtles. That was... a little while back? I had the most adorable little grandchildren in the world. One loved to draw coral, the second loved exploring mazes, and my last grandbaby always got lost, no matter where he was."

The eel had a faraway, dreamy look in her eyes as she continued her story.

"Anyway, my grandchildren were visiting and they started wandering around, the thing all youngsters do. I had fallen asleep thanks to my aching bones and when I woke up, they were gone. I looked everywhere, and happened to take a look inside a dark hole…"

The eel shivered.

A dark hole? I wondered. Did that sound familiar?

Then the answer beaned me on the head.

"I ventured in. I was nervous for my grandchildren's safety, but otherwise I would never go in that dang hole." The eel spat, shaking her head.

"There were some dark things in there, yes. I didn't find out till I was smack in the very center of the path. The sunlight didn't reach me, but I kept going. Suddenly some figure jumped in front of me. It shocked me to the bone, and of course, I electrified it on instinct. The animal collapsed, but it seemed another one of its pals happened to be nearby. That animal got upset and-and-and…"

The eel shook her head, her eyes growing glassy.

"It cursed me. Cursed me and sent me into the Coral Maze. With ease, I found my way out and started to leave. But a strange magic bound me to the Coral Maze. Each time I attempted to leave it, I was sucked back into the Coral Maze."

Pity filled my chest.

"I can't pass the Circle of Coral. And my sole job is to prank and test any creature who dares venture in the Coral Maze."

The eel grimaced.

"Oh, no!" I exclaimed, cupping my hands to my mouth. "I have a question…"

"Go with the current."

"Earlier I saw a circle of coral outside the Coral Maze. Is that the Coral Circle?"

"Yes, that is the Coral Circle." The eel nodded solemnly.

"So… after you save Maui, I must ask if you could also break my curse?"

"I will try my best." I vowed.

I explained everything that had happened before my friends and I had met the eel.

"Lydia placed her hand on the Coral Maze, trembled, and fell over! We carried her over to a kelp patch and started inside the Coral Maze." I finished.

"I had a hunch, though I didn't want to believe it." The eel shook her head.

"Darling, this is bad. If the Coral Maze dies, so does Lydia. If-if Lydia d-d-dies, will you take these seeds to a trustworthy mermaid?"

The eel looked as worried about Lydia as a mother would react about a lost child.

"Of course. I will do my best. As well as for Lydia, don't give up hope." I said, accepting the bag of seeds from Eel.

"Who cursed you?"

The eel looked at me, surprised by my bluntness.

"Sorry, I'm not trying to be rude." I quickly corrected myself.

"But, if I know who cursed you, I might be able to find the correct antidote to help you. I mean, whatever has been done with magic can be undone!"

"Oh, it's fine, dear!" The eel paused. "But the creature that cursed me was large and bulky."

"But let me give you the full scene. There was a merman behind the creature, and he was laughing, saying to me that I would bear the curse of ... some name I forgot... Sla or something, I think it was."

I gasped. "Any more details?"

"Nope. I couldn't see him very clearly 'cuz it was dark. Power emitted from him." The eel shook her head.

"Oh." My mind whirled.

Was it just me, or had the eel said SLA? Sla was close to Slate.

I opened my mouth to say something, then stopped as eel interrupted me.

"But back to the present. Good job. None have ever made it to the center of the Coral Maze before. Other than me and Lydia, of course…"

"Thanks." I smiled.

"Honey, you and your friends have the greatest stamina and most grit I've ever seen!" The eel praised me. I shyly twirled a strand of black hair.

"Secretly, I suspect you feed on stamina and grit, honesty." The eel joked.

I laughed. "I better catch up with my friends now." I sadly pouted. "I only wish you could come with us to the Friendship Point."

"Oh, don't fret your fins." The eel chuckled.

"I'm coming with you all the way to the very edge of the Coral Circle."

"Great!" I exclaimed.

The eel nodded in agreement.

"It's better with company when strolling through a huge, daunting maze after all, hm?"

"Yes." I nodded.

"Oh, and careful, honey." The eel quickly added. "Some of my old-old-old traps are still around here. Most are by the entrance of the Coral Maze. Actually, a good variety of 'em."

I sighed. "I'll watch out for them. After all, itching dust doesn't sound very appealing."

Chapter 19

DEATH OF A FRIEND

Screams pierced the water and I swam closer to the maze's entrance, the eel close behind.

"Get your hairy leg off of me! You, ARGH!" a voice I identified as Faith shrieked.

What happened?

Who was Faith yelling at?

I hurried towards the entrance of the Coral Maze and peeked around the corner.

"Oh no! Olivia! Let go of her!" Faith was yelling.

My jaw dropped to the ground.

Giant spiders were fighting Faith furiously.

They wore a blank expression and had thin legs that didn't look like they could hold themselves up.

And next to them was my BFFs, Olivia, and Lily all tied up while my other BFF Faith was in trouble.

A figure stood behind Olivia and Lily, watching the battle through cold, narrowed eyes.

And the worst part?

That "figure" was Slate of Chaos!

Blood clotted around his cheeks, and he wore a black mask, though I could make out a pointed nose and crooked teeth.

Slate wore a black suit with scarlet drops splattered all over it, and his boots were white.

Slate swam over to the Circle of Coral and perched on top.

He ordered for Olivia and Lily to be set down there, along with their Friendship stones.

Olivia and Lily's Friendship stones rode on the back of the biggest spider of them all, who set them onto the ground at Slate's feet.

Olivia and Lily were struggling madly, but they were bound to each other so tightly it took even a great effort to budge.

Faith was clutching her stone and she was busy kicking at a spider who had her leg clamped in its jaws.

She punched a spider who was sniffing at her hair.

But there were too many spiders, and with great fear I knew the crowd of spiders would overwhelm Faith.

The eel sidled to my side to see what was happening and gaped, her jaw hanging.

But she wasn't looking at Faith.

She was looking at Slate of Chaos, as if she had seen him before.

And with growing dread, I knew she had.

"Grab her stone!" Slate ordered. "Now!"

"Not a chance!" Faith shot at Slate, but a large burly spider was holding her tightly.

Olivia and Lily cheered as Faith threw many retorts at Slate, but Lily's voice was quickly muffled as a spider gagged her.

"Stop wiggling, fairy!" Slate was yelling to Faith.

"Never, Slate!" Faith exclaimed. "You won't win, you evil, um, demon-hearted villain!"

She didn't even tremble, confident with her precious stone.

"STOP!" shrieked Slate.

"Now it's clear why I LOATHE, DESPISE, DETEST, and HATE HAPPY LITTLE IDIOTIC STUPID FAIRIES!" he bellowed at Faith, and a few of his army spiders turned away from him and shuddered.

The same burly spider held Faith out to Slate, Faith's friendship stone wedged underneath her arm.

Slate pried it from her, and cackled, "MINE!"

I gasped.

"NO!" Faith screamed, lunging forward. "My Friendship Stone!"

A spider tied her, quickly wrapping long spiderweb around her in her moment of stillness.

"Spider webs?" Faith cried incredulously. "As binds?" she tried to break free, but the spider web held, not even budging.

"Ha!" Slate growled. "MY giant spider ARMY produces spider webs unlike any other!"

"STOP!" Faith protested but was quickly gagged and set down next to Olivia and Lily.

"FAITH!" Olivia screamed but was gagged quickly. "MMMMMM!"

What could I do to help my friends?

I searched for a plan, an idea, anything that would free my friends and defeat Slate.

But I knew what Slate would do.

Slate was going to destroy the Friendship stones and it would be bye-bye to Maui before I could do anything to stop him.

But I couldn't just hide here like some-some-cowardly-coward!

My friends were in danger!

"They were ambushed!" I gritted my teeth. "My friends were ambushed by Slate of Chaos! That's what the black dots were on my map! Slate. And his spiders!"

"Spiders? The black things are spiders?" The eel murmured distractedly. "I feel the power coming off of that wingless fairy in great waves."

I uneasily shuffled my feet. "Eel, I've been meaning to tell you… Slate cursed you. Slate of Chaos. Him."

"Slate?" The eel growled under her breath.

"It all makes sense now. Look at those black, skinny creatures, the spider things! They are the ones who confronted me when I was in that hole! And Slate of Chaos stood behind, laughing as he CURSED ME!"

I quickly shushed the eel.

She was fuming with rage.

Her fins quivered and she shook in anger.

I swiftly flattened myself to the coral, then quickly pulled away as it started to creak.

The eel glared at the spiders through narrowed eyes before darting back to hide.

"What was that?" Slate yelled to particularly no one.

But then he looked at Faith, who was still hissing like crazy. Slate turned to a spider.

"I thought the gags actually worked."

"The others are quiet." Whispered the spider nervously. "We can get another gag."

Faith was attempting to chew through her gag and made a face of disgust, yowling loudly.

Whoever had gagged Faith didn't do it properly.

Thunk!

Slate had kicked the spider on the kneecap. It looked ready to bowl over.

"See that you do find a good gag." Slate hissed curtly before turning away.

He walked into the wasteland and the gloomy water around the Coral Maze. "What a wonder. What a sight. How much despair lurks around. How delicious. I smell the trouble and chaos."

He took a deep breath, then walked over to a spot with a small dot of sunshine shone through the water.

"Begone!" Slate cried and waved his gloved hand.

The sunlight lolled into his open palm and he crushed it with glee.

When he opened his hand, all that was left of the joyful sunlight was pure shadow.

The eel gritted her teeth angrily, and I could imagine smoke coming off her head.

"NOOO!" Olivia yelled, startling Slate.

She had somehow chewed through her gag.

"HELP! HELP! HELP! HELP! And gimme my Friendship stone! HELP!"

Olivia's screams echoed off the Coral Maze and they shook tremendously, surprising the eel as it backed up into my face.

"YOU!" Slate beckoned the spider he had kicked earlier to step forward.

I didn't look.

There was a horrible scream, and a black corpse collapsed onto the ground.

Slate's white gloves were now stained red.

The blood mixed with the murky water and I shuddered.

"Ha! That's what the gag spider got for not doing his job properly!" Slate cackled, then looked at Olivia's chewed gag.

He glanced at the crowd of spiders.

"Who wants to be the next gag spider?"

No movement.

Slate rolled his eyes.

"Me, the hardworking lad! The only one who knows how to do EVERYTHING!"

"Oh, then! Do you know how to lose?" Olivia glared at him. "If not, I'll teach you a lesson!"

Slate pretended to yawn. "How boring. Such impulsive remarks from your big mouth!"

He clapped his hands, and a wave of dark purple magic swirled around a startled Olivia, who tried to bite it as it formed into a purple gag over her mouth.

"There. That's better, no more noise!"

I had a sickening feeling in my stomach.

The eel waved its tail and swam around another corner.

I followed, but I didn't want to leave my friends behind without knowing what would happen to them.

"Let's destroy the Friendship stones, shall we?"

I froze.

There was a loud clunk and Slate yelled like a maniac.

"Execute the weapons spider who brought me this useless stainless-steel axe that failed to destroy the Friendship stones!"

A wail echoed off the walls and someone screamed.

"I will destroy you, stone! Darkness will flood Maui, and I shall stand supreme! And before that, who wants to be the new weapons spider, hmm?"

NO!

Slate was destroying the Friendship stones!

I groaned softly and the eel slapped its tail across my mouth.

"Oh, Eel, what do I do?" I had come up with a name for the eel.

Eel.

How fitting to be an eel and to be called Eel.

I hugged Eel as she patted my back with her tail.

"There, there." Eel whispered, biting her fin in worry, though she was having a hard time keeping her anger in check.

"Calm down and clear your mind. Oh, when I get my fins on Slate, I'll-I'll…"

I nodded and we swam back towards Slate.

"You! DUMB! Little! STONE!" Slate took the green Friendship stone and flung it into the dull basalt pebbles lying on the dirty seafloor.

"WHY DON'T YOU BREAK?!?!?!"

Lily shook as her stone bounced off the pebbles.

"Um, Sire, the Friendship stones are very strong." Stammered a spider with a thick book open.

"They are made for this purpose, so you can't accidentally drop it and break it, or destroy it in one of your rages. Perhaps Commander Crusher-" he motioned to the biggest spider. "Might be able to crush the Friendship stones?"

Commander Crusher was the burly spider that had held Faith out to Slate, and he had muscles bulging out from his body.

Commander Crusher!

I remembered the Flying Fairies newspaper I had seen earlier, in the article about Commander Crusher.

Crusher was eagerly waiting for his turn to break the Friendship stones.

"SILENCE! AND DON'T SAY THAT WORD! Soon, Maui will forget the word 'friendship' has ever existed!" Slate whistled, glaring at the spider who had spoken.

Slate formed balls of dark magic and began pelting the spider. "If I can't break the Friendship stones, no one can!"

"Please, sir! OW! Please... Ow! Uh! Ow! I'll do anything!"

Slate gave him a stony look and bared his teeth.

"See that you never say the word 'friendship' EVER again." He whistled again, this time the pitch of his voice dropped.

The balls of dark magic vanished.

Slate muttered to himself, his gaze sweeping over the Coral Maze.

I froze as his eyes came to rest next to where I was crouched.

Faith blinked at Slate with wide eyes. Though beneath her gag, I could make out a stiff chin and bared teeth.

Commander Crusher swam forward and glared down at my friends.

"Now Slate is going to take over Maui! And everyone has to bow down to him or die!" Crusher smirked at Faith's horrified expression.

"Right, Slate of Chaos? We'll rule Maui!"

"No, you idiot!" Slate hit Commander Crusher on the head.

"I thought you were smarter than all the other spiders like you claimed to be!"

"I am." Commander Crusher croaked, rubbing his head. He looked utterly confused, and so was I.

WHAT? I thought. *Taking over Maui was not Slate's ultimate plan? Fluttering fairies! Then what IS his master plan?*

"Why Maui, everyone asks?" Slate started. "Why is the Friendship Point in Maui? Many have wondered. Well, wonder no more! I, the great, supreme, awesome, marvelous-"

"Get to the point!" Commander Crusher interrupted.

Slate glared at him and socked him in the stomach. Crusher bowled over in pain.

"Anyway, I, Slate of Chaos, will unveil the mystery!" Slate declared.

Commander Crusher and the rest of the spiders just blinked in more confusion.

"Legend says that Maui is the CENTER of Friendship. Yes, you heard me right." Slate chuckled unpleasantly.

Faith, Olivia, and Lily wrinkled their brows cluelessly.

"Maui is the center of Friendship?" Commander Crusher stated.

Eel inhaled nervously and arched one perfect eyebrow.

Slate continued his "lesson", sending pointed glances at Commander Crusher.

"When I destroy the Friendship stones, darkness will fall upon everyone. Then Haleakala the massive volcano will erupt!"

Haleakala?

I wondered, then realized it was the same volcano I saw while on the beach with my friends earlier.

"Plumes of smoke will cover the sky, drowning out the sun, and lava will flood Maui. Everyone in Maui will perish!"

Slate hissed, lowering his voice ominously.

A spider started playing creepy music on a flute. Another spider turned on a fan.

Olivia gasped, and I stared at Slate in disbelief.

"I'll leave Maui to be consumed by the lava!" Slate giggled darkly. "Who cares about Maui? Not me!"

"And with Maui gone, the world will be terribly weakened without the center of Friendship." Slate cackled.

"And I will rule the world!"

He turned to the Friendship stones, and I knew immediately what he was going to do next.

"Now it's time to destroy Friendship! The first step in my take-over-the-world-plan!"

Ash fell as a great boulder was lifted into the air and was prepared to be hurled at the Friendship stones.

"Spiders!" Slate yelled.

"Please step aside unless you want to get crushed. Although that would work too. A pool of blood would look nice."

The cluster of spiders shuffled to the side.

NO!

Even the Friendship stones couldn't stand such a heavy rock!

I gasped, turning to Eel. "What should we do? The Friendship Stones will be destroyed before we even have a chance to save Friendship!"

"AND the world will end as we know it!" I added.

"Eel?" I whispered, starting up.

Eel wasn't next to me anymore.

I looked around anxiously. Where did she go?

Then I saw something that made my heart stop.

Eel was rocketing towards Slate.

Her eyes glinted with determination.

Eel bared her fangs.

Electricity flowed down her spine as she neared.

I gasped in horror and dread.

Eel was - attacking Slate!

No one heard my gasp, for they were all petrified by the great boulder, everyone except Slate, who was cackling like crazy, unable to stop.

Eel rammed into Slate at full force.

Fresh waves of electricity flowed down her spine and into a shocked Slate.

Slate jolted up, and Eel continuously zapped bolt after bolt of electricity into Slate.

BOOM!

Slate dropped the boulder onto the ground, a wingspan away from tied up Faith, Olivia, and Lily.

I shuddered, readying myself to pull Eel out of the fray.

"STOP!" Eel glared at Slate. "I'm not going to sugarcoat my words."

"What you are doing is wrong. The inhabitants of Maui need Friendship, and so does the world. You cannot destroy Friendship!"

Eel hissed venomously at Slate.

What was Eel doing?

She was putting herself in grave danger!

I started forward to pull her out of the mess, but I tripped on a long piece of kelp.

Suddenly, long strands of kelp and dirty seaweed were launched from all sides. They covered me from my wings to the tips of my boots and it felt like I was being glued to the ground.

This must be one of the Eel's pranks she set a long time ago!

I grimaced as itching dust powdered my face and the rotting seaweed and kelp left sludges of slime on my cheeks.

I struggled wildly but the kelp didn't budge.

I wanted to scream, but I didn't want to attract the attention of Slate.

My hair was caught in the coral now, and I was bound on the ground, wiggling like a beached fish.

Did you know that coral is as hard as rock and is very tangled?

My head hurt and my fingers reached for my pocket knife.

I heard a snap from Eel as she hissed at Slate.

"Oh look!" Slate jeered at Eel, seeming to recover from his electric shock.

"A hero. I must ask, why are you so eager to meet your doom?" he cocked his head and pretended to think. "Maybe because you're as stupid as a sea slug!"

He pointed his finger at Eel. "Good-bye!"

A jet of light streaked out, but the Eel was faster.

She dodged it, swerved around Slate, and electrified him again.

I struggled and hacked at the kelp some more, though my eyes kept darting to Eel's progress.

"Stop THE EEL!" Slate screamed to Commander Crusher, who repeated it eagerly to his spiders.

"YES, stop THE EEL!" Commander Crusher screamed to his spiders, who lunged forward at Eel.

Eel shocked a spider and twisted around the leg of the next. She stunned two spiders and whisked up into the water, swimming over the spiders' heads.

Row after row of spiders jumped forward in coordination, each aiming for a part of Eel's body to grip onto.

Eel electrified them with a wave of her tail, breaking free, and snatched a Friendship stone from the ground in her mouth.

But it was knocked from her mouth.

Eel quickly picked up a sharp stone and hacked at the rope around my friends. But she had to quickly swim away as a spider pursed her.

Eel dived down, trying to grab the other Friendship stones. Commander Crusher, seeming to know her next move, gripped her tail.

He waved Eel around mockingly.

I gasped in horror and shushed myself, straining to hear what Slate was saying.

"You come from the Coral Maze?" Slate watched Eel as she electrified Commander Crusher.

Still, Commander Crusher did not let go of her tail, instead, tightened his grip.

"You were the stupid eel that wandered into my old base, weren't you?"

"Yes, I ventured inside a hole!" Eel growled, thrashing in Crusher's grip.

She twisted around and bit into Crusher's claw. "Is there something wrong with that?"

Commander Crusher yowled in fury, shaking his claw, and thumped Eel against the ground.

Eel refused to yelp in pain. She dug her teeth in deeper.

Slate cocked his head, looking hungry as blood streamed from Eel's side.

"That hole is the entrance to my old base. My scuba spiders happened to find you wandering aimlessly in there. I wasn't going to let them take all the fun!"

Eel struggled against Crusher's claws. "That's your idea of fun?"

Electricity flowed from her spine down to Crusher's claws. Commander Crusher collapsed in a daze.

Eel sped forward, fangs outstretched, aiming for Slate.

Slate quickly caught her and held the struggling eel by the head.

I muffled a screech of anger.

"Oh! This is for cursing me! This is for Lydia!" Eel ranted, and electrified Slate.

"This is for Friendship and the world!"

Slate wrinkled his brow, sweat beads rolling down his forehead, and tightened his grip on Eel.

"And this is for the Coral Maze!" Eel hissed, whacking him in the face with her tail.

Slate spat on her as Eel continued.

"When your darkness spread, it chose the wrong place to infest!"

Eel twisted and her jaws clasped Slate's thumb. "And this is for booby-trapping the fairies with a Cursed Key!"

Slate slapped her, and a wave of dark magic encased Eel, freezing her.

He then turned to my friends. "Did you see what I left for you stinking fairies? The Cursed Key, the thing this slug mentioned! Too bad someone broke it. It was the cleverest manipulating evil-magic object EVER!"

Lily's eyes widened. Gold had been right; the 'S' symbol on the key meant Slate.

"I knew it was you!" Eel murmured in her frozen position.

"A slug like you doesn't deserve to know about my key!" Slate rolled his eyes at Eel.

"Actually, I'm a moray eel!"

"Really?" Slate frowned, cocking his head. "Eel, slug. All the same."

"You won't destroy Friendship!" Eel gasped.

Her tail had been awkwardly frozen, and her jaw hung open, fangs still bared.

"This is for the sake of Friendship! Friendship will flourish!"

"Oh, yeah? There's nothing a slug like you can do to stop me!" Slate snickered, and passed Eel to Crusher.

Commander Crusher caught it and held Eel out for Slate.

Slate pointed a finger at her. "Say bye to the world, you slimy moray eel! And meet the death beam!"

From his fingertip a jet of violet lightning twirled towards the struggling Eel.

Eel tried to twist out of the way, but was helpless. She was frozen.

I felt numb as the beam of light neared.

POW!

And in a blink of the eye, it was over.

I gazed meekly at the utterly still body.

Eel's eyes were spread wide open, and her tail was wrenched in an awkward angle.

With a grunt, Crusher kicked Eel towards the Coral Maze.

I stared in disbelief as Eel's cold body collided into the tiki pole and sank to the dusty ground.

She was dead.

Chapter 20
THE FRIENDSHIP POINT

Grief and sorrow welled up inside of me as I stared at Eel's body.

I couldn't believe it - I wish it wasn't true - Eel was dead.

I then looked towards the murderer.

Slate of Chaos.

I wanted to strangle him.

I wanted to punish him.

He was pure evil.

EVIL. I couldn't let a person like this rule the world!

NEVER!

But first, I had to untangle myself from the kelp and seaweed containing me.

And I also had to keep an ear perked for any clues, and perhaps possible weaknesses Slate had.

"HA!" Slate cackled loudly, and I snatched a peek at what was happening.

His spiders looked at him blankly, and Slate waved his arm.

That sent the spiders barking with laughter.

"That lousy eel was stupid to think it could overcome me, Slate of Chaos!" Slate bragged. "And my magic is so strong! My death beam killed the eel on impact!"

HEY! Eel is NOT lousy! You are! I gritted my teeth.

Faith, Olivia, and Lily's eyes were darting from Slate to Eel's limp body in terror.

Slate turned to the boulder and glanced at the Friendship stones lying on the ground.

"Now, now. Let's continue the destruction of Friendship, shall we? Friendship stones, meet your DEATH!"

A blur of gray hurled at the Friendship stones. The crowd of spiders leaned away from Slate and the boulder, preparing themselves for the impact.

CRACK!

I gasped as smoke poured over the clearing from the boulder's power.

NO!

I gulped and waited for darkness to shroud the clearing even more, as the Friendship stones were being destroyed.

I lay on the cold sea floor, not even attempting to free myself from the seaweed.

I was too scared to look at the heaps of broken-up rock the Friendship stones would become, or even pure powder!

I knew darkness and evil were rising at this very moment.

But I felt nothing, not even the touch of darkness on my skin.

Is it possible?

An angry yowl rang in my ears as I tore at the seaweed surrounding me.

"THIS-THIS- "

"It didn't work!" gasped a spider.

The spiders were talking among themselves and muttering darkly, glancing at the overjoyed Friendship fairies every few seconds.

I rolled to the side for a better view, shocked at what I found.

Why were Faith, Olivia, and Lily happy – wait, could it be?

I scanned the clearing.

I couldn't inspect the Friendship stones closely from my distance but I knew they were still intact.

On the other wing, the big boulder had crumpled into a million little pieces, not that I was counting.

I whispered, *YES!!!!,* although I said it to myself so Slate wouldn't hear.

Slate furrowed his brow, looking tensely at the Friendship stones.

He picked up Faith's rosy Friendship stone.

"There is a strong magic protecting the Friendship stones from harm's way. A revolting, familiar magic…"

He twirled it in his fingers and suddenly dropped the stone, yelping as if it had burned him.

"The Friendship Point enchantment!" Slate seethed.

He paused, ignoring the fact that his white glove was dripping red with blood.

"But no need to waste my time with the Friendship Fairies. If I destroy the Friendship Point, the Friendship stone and Friendship Fairies will be gone forever."

Slate narrowed his eyes into slits.

"No more Friendship to weaken me. And I will RULE THE WORLD!"

"YES! Slate will RULE THE WORLD!" Commander Crusher yowled.

His spiders nodded vigorously and cheered, stirring up a wave.

Faith whimpered. Lily sniffled. Olivia sat there, dazed.

Slate? Rule the world? I wailed inwardly. *I'd much rather let an ant rule the world rather than Slate!*

"Don't worry," Slate turned to Faith, Olivia, and Lily. "You are no use to me anymore."

Faith exhaled.

"But. I have a better way to dispose of you." Slate's yellow eyes glowed an evil shade of ultraviolet.

Faith held her breath.

Slate's lip curled upwards towards his sunken eyes, and his very skin seemed to radiate with power.

"I will leave you three here. You have eaten The Breath of the Sea, which enables you to breathe underwater. But only for a limited time period. Soon you will choke and try to hold your breath as The Breath of the Sea's power runs out. Water will invade your lungs and suffocate you!" Slate scornfully smiled.

Olivia shrank back.

"And the last thing you will see before you die is the body of the dead eel!" Slate whispered.

Lily stole a glance at Eel.

"Oh! I'm so evil! The thought of you dying so slowly in agony makes me laugh!" Slate cackled.

"Mwa-ha-ha-ha! Mwa-ha-ha!"

Faith huddled closer to her friends, Olivia stared at him defyingly and almost helplessly, and Lily looked ready to faint.

I clenched my teeth, feeling so hot I could burn through my kelp and seaweed bindings.

How DARE Slate threaten my friends?

Just they wait until I got my hands-on Slate and his measly spiders!

I glared at Slate. If looks could kill, the great Slate of Chaos would be dead.

Slate turned to three spiders who were clustered over a map.

One chortled in a language I didn't know. It was full of grunts and deep bellows.

"It takes THAT long to get to the Friendship Point?" Slate fumed, then he relaxed.

"But with my magic, we'll get there in no time."

The spider nodded and timidly bowed. Slate huffed, impatiently tapping his foot against the seafloor.

"To the surface! Last one there will get a sample of my magic!" Slate ordered to the rest of the spiders.

"Bye, Friendship Flies. I'm off to rule the world and destroy Friendship!"

"To the surface!" Commander Crusher repeated to the rest of the spiders. "Bye, Friendship Flies! We're going to destroy Friendship!"

He was clearly learning ways to insult from his lord Slate of Chaos.

The spiders swam to the surface. From there I made out a storm cloud hovering at the surface of the ocean.

The spiders leaped onto the cloud, and they were whisked away.

I made sure they were out of sight as I untangled myself from the last pieces of kelp and seaweed strapping me down.

Standing up, I looked sadly at Eel's motionless body.

Then I rushed to my friends.

I swam to Faith's side and began hacking at the spider web around her. "I was tangled up earlier in kelp and seaweed."

"GGG!" Faith motioned to her gag.

"Oh, right. The gag. Sorry."

I untied the gag for Faith, and she let out a big breath. "Thanks, Pia! We have to stop Slate! I won't let a vile sewer rat like him rule the world…"

"Agreed." I untied the spider webs.

I removed the gags from Olivia.

I glanced back at Eel's lifeless body and untied Lily's gag. "He murdered Eel!"

"The poor eel!" Lily wailed.

Using my sharp pocket knife, I freed Olivia and Lily from the black rope and they stood up, dusting themselves off.

Faith bent down and stuffed something into her Wing-on.

I paused, sadly gazing at the limp body of Eel out of the corner of my eyes.

Only, it seemed, a few wingbeats ago it had been filled with life, hope, and love.

"Let's have a moment of silence for noble Eel, who died trying to stop Slate and took out many spiders in the process."

I whispered, bowing my head to Eel.

Faith, Olivia, and Lily bowed too, tears streaking down their faces.

"She was very brave today." Faith murmured.

"Eel had a good sense of humor," Olivia whispered.

"Eel helped us find Faith in the Coral Maze when we thought she was lost forever." Lily cried.

I sniffed, rubbing my tears on my arm.

"When we save Friendship and the world today, it will be in Eel's honor." I declared respectfully, standing up.

"Now where is the Friendship Point?" I asked Faith.

"The beach." Faith looked at me, though her eyes kept wandering to Eel's body.

"Come on." I shot up towards the surface of the water, Faith hot on my trail.

Faith was thinking hard, looking like she would burst into tears any second.

Lily was dabbing her eyes with a handkerchief, and Olivia sucked in her cheeks.

I looked back at the small figure lying prone on the seafloor.

It hurt to leave the Eel behind - but we had no other choice.

We broke through the surface of the water with one big splash and looked around.

The sky was darkening, and we probably didn't have much time before sunset.

"This way." I fell back and let Faith take the lead.

"Have you been to the Friendship Point before?" I asked Faith curiously, trying to make conversation.

"Nope." Faith answered, her eyes on the road. "Oh! Just in case, Pia, you might want to know about that very obvious trail Slate must have left behind."

Faith pointed at the blood trail in the water.

I retched in realization as I saw a spider's skinny limb stick out of the water and flail wildly before sinking out of sight.

No one said anything after that.

I shivered as we stumbled across another giant spider's corpse floating on the water.

Was Slate drowning his spiders because of a small mistake they had made, or was he murdering them merely for his own fun?

I shivered, which was replaced by a fresh wave of confidence.

We would defeat Slate of Chaos and save Friendship.

For Eel. For Buttercup.

I collided into Faith.

She had slowed down and was heading into the dense forest behind the Friendship Point.

There was a "Heave! Ho! Slate's going to rule the world! Heave! Ho!" as we neared, determined to stop Slate.

I shuffled closer to the source of the noise and peeked through the dense foundation of plants and climbing up onto a tree with tangled branches.

I squinted and leaned onto a branch to get a better view, my friends perching silently in different places.

Slate had set his spiders to work.

The spiders were holding big rocks and pounding them against the three stands.

"Chant!" Commander Crusher was demanding. "Chanting helps you work harder! Chant! Wait, did I already say that?"

The spiders half-heartedly chanted loudly, "Heave! Ho! Slate's going to rule the world!"

"Oh my!" I moaned quietly, eyeing the mass of spiders.

"Slate has even more spiders here!"

"How come we didn't see them earlier?" Olivia wondered.

"Because they were probably waiting on land for orders," Lily answered.

"Hand the book over!" Slate demanded. Then he gleefully giggled.

"Oh, I can't WAIT till I get to rule the world! Imagine!"

A plump spider held up a book, and Slate seized it, shifting his heavy chest-piece, and started reading.

"Blah, blah, blah…… Not this page…"

I leaned closer.

"It's not highly recommended to fool around or test the Friendship Point. Like that's going to happen to the great Slate of Chaos!"

The spider beside him vigorously nodded.

"That stupid library is better without books on Friendship! But it is useful to know, I admit…"

Slate muttered darkly. "When I rule the world, I will get a grand, evil, dark palace and perhaps a library with some spell books…"

I shuddered.

"Fluttering Fairies!" Faith breathed, spotting a glimmer of reflected light.

249

"There's my Friendship stone! I can almost reach it…."

"What are these?" Commander Crusher asked, poking a pole.

"If you had done your homework and actually bothered to read the reports, you would know what the Friendship Point looked like."

Slate hissed, tossing the book aside. "You can start now." He threw a pile of papers at Crusher.

Commander Crusher growled under his breath but said no more.

"Move!" Slate barked, and walked over to one of the Friendship stands.

The spiders backed up quickly as if they knew what was happening.

RUSTLE!

Lily stumbled on the branch she was sitting on, being forced back by a bee.

"Who's there?" Slate turned around.

We froze. The bee froze and buzzed away.

"Is it those pesky 'Friendship Failures'?" Slate hissed, eyes flicking over the bushes.

His scorching eyes passed several times over us.

We stiffly stood there in a panic.

Spiders started crawling around, their skinny bodies covered the floor as they scanned for any "Friendship Failures".

Slate stuck his nose into the air and turned away, leaving his spiders to do the searching themselves.

Faith placed a hand on my shoulders, surprising me.

She whispered rapidly in my ear. I passed the message on to the others, and they trembled but nodded.

I hoped Faith's plan would work.

I gave one last hug to Faith, then slowly flew to my spot as the others did so too, admiring the fine scenery of the Friendship Point.

Ocean waves lapped at the shore by the Friendship Point. Seagulls squawked, seeing the giant spiders, and flew away.

The Friendship Point looked like a temple in my opinion.

The pearly white ground reflected sunlight onto the stone in the center of the Friendship Point.

The stone was a mix of pink, green, and blue. It was called the 'Anuenue pohaku', which was referred to as the 'Rainbow stone'.

Surrounding the Rainbow stone were the three Friendship stands.

Above it, supported by three white poles, the crown ring stood glistening proudly, holding a large pink crystal.

The large crystal was called the 'Aloha no aniani' – the 'Friendship Fire crystal'.

I couldn't wait to save Friendship and see the Friendship stones in action.

My friends would set the Friendship stones on the Friendship stands.

Then Friendship energy would go from the Friendship stones to the Rainbow stone in the center.

The Rainbow stone would combine the energy and send it to the Friendship Fire crystal.

The Friendship Fire crystal would then spread the Friendship across the world.

My head whirled from all the information.

The Friendship energy goes from the Friendship stones to the Rainbow stone in the

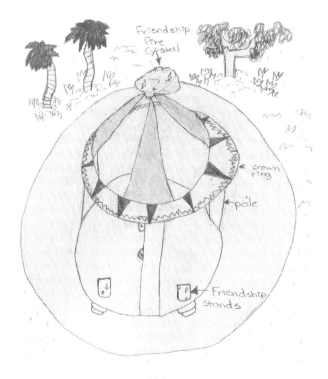

middle, and then to the Friendship fire crystal on top.

I thought, just to make it simple for my confused brain.

But the important part: the Friendship fairies need to keep their hands on the Friendship stone, and channel the Friendship energy.

I got this. WE got this.

I gulped as the time to take out our plan grew near.

The world was in our shaking hands.

Taking a breath, I made the signal.

"NOW!" I screamed.

I flew up, seeing my friends rise with me for a split second. Faith, Olivia, and Lily dove for their stones without hesitation.

I aimed for Slate.

Slate whipped around and I leaped on top of him. His eyes widened. I yelled, punching him in the face.

"I thought I sensed Friendship scum!" Slate growled, backing away from me.

Fury blinded my senses as Slate punched me in the stomach. I gasped, glaring at him as a fresh wave of pain flooded my nerves.

I threw a nice jab at his chest as I pinned him down.

Slate threw me back with a hiss, then glanced at his spiders. I followed his gaze.

They were clustered around the Friendship stones, and Commander Crusher was howling orders at the spiders.

"Circle position!" Crusher yelped as Faith dove in for her stone. "Pinchers at the ready!" Commander Crusher commanded, and his claw darted up, hooking Olivia's shirt.

Something thumped me in the head.

Feeling lightheaded, I scolded myself before barreling into Slate. *That's what you get for being distracted!*

We tussled around and around, and I made sure to throw a few extra punches.

A feeling of exhilaration shook my body.

"I don't think I had the chance to introduce myself!" Slate drawled, swiping his leg.

"I'm Slate of Chaos! If it wasn't obvious. I mean, the gold chest plate, the black suit, white gloves…"

"The name's Pia!" I punched him in the chest piece. Clang! The metal sound rang in my ears.

I withdrew a bruised fist.

"OH! That's what I forgot about!" Slate realized, smirking. "I forgot the cowardly Pine fairy. That's you."

"The name's Pia the Pinena fairy!" I dove at Slate and he dodged easily, toying with me.

"Ah, foolish fairy!" Slate mocked, showing his skill as he caught my leg mid-kick.

"Don't call me that!" I pulled my leg back.

"Then what should I call you, an arrogant flea? Though that DOES suit you very much." Slate rolled his eyes, and I took the opportunity to jab my elbow into his stomach.

He didn't even flinch.

Slate glared at me through eyes full of venom. "Don't get your hopes up, fairy. You just dug your own grave."

My wings batted the air as I flew towards him, feeling as strong enough to summon a tornado.

But before I could do anything, Slate backed up, then jumped onto a nearby lightning cloud and rose into the air.

I threw a water bubble at him, relishing the cool feeling of the water in my palms before hurling more.

Behind me, I heard yells, and a thud as a spider fell to the ground in shock.

"You have been a nuisance." Slate growled at me, snapping me to the cry of battle.

He formed a black ball with purple streaks.

I felt like if I stared into it, I would be sucked in and never come back out.

Slate's face contorted into a purely evil grin as he lifted the ball.

"Say your prayers!" the ball whizzed into the air, and I dodged it just in time, feeling it burn my hair.

"FIRE!" I screamed. My hair was indeed on fire.

Forming water bubbles, I drenched my head.

"Oh, how embarrassing for you!" Slate cackled.

I barely had time to register what Slate had just said, as my ears picked up a whooshing sound.

"Wha-?" I turned around.

The black ball had doubled back and was a wingspan away from me.

I dropped to the ground, but not fast enough.

My forehead burned. I felt blood trickle down.

Drops of blood were dripping from my right ear where it had grazed it.

I hoped my injury wasn't deep and stumbled on my feet, feeling woozy.

Blood from my forehead trickled over my right eye and I desperately tried to blink it away.

I could see the ball of dark magic in the distance.

Stamina. Grit. I'll pull through. Won't I?

"Like my Orb of Death?" Slate laughed, eyeing my blood with thirst, as if he was a vampire.

And he might be one.

"It takes complicated magic to make an Orb of Death, fairy!" Slate cackled.

"Enjoy my hard work, for I have enough dark magic to make FOUR Orbs of Death!"

I groaned and stuck out my tongue in response.

The Orb of Death streaked towards me, and the grass withered and the palm trees wilted as the ball flew past them.

I had a second to come up with a good fool-proof plan to get rid of the orb.

So, what did I know about the Orb? I knew it would follow me wherever I went.

And I also knew how to take advantage of that.

Circling a tree, I quickly flew up and shot towards Slate.

The Death Ball chasing me followed quickly, starting a wildfire on the sparse grass.

The orb was flying too fast to stop. Perfect.

"Hey!" Slate yelped, backing up.

I was flying like a rocket towards him. *Closer, Closer, Close…*

Slate's eyes widened in surprise as I suddenly swerved to the side.

The Orb of Death behind me slowed, trying to avoid Slate, but it was flying too fast.

"You!" Slate growled, thrusting his hand forward in a shield.

The Death ball behind me collided into Slate. KA-POW!

Smoke clouded over the place Slate had been standing.

I hopefully stared into the smoke.

Faith, Olivia, and Lily glanced over. The spiders froze.

Silence filled the clearing.

My heart was bursting with joy.

Butterflies nervously flitted in and about my stomach.

All the spiders cowered in fear beneath Faith, Olivia, and Lily.

We had won, and vanquished Slate of Chaos!

The world was saved from his evil grasp!

Commander Crusher grunted to break the silence.

"Slate!" he yelped, not sounding particularly enthusiastic. He took on an annoyed tone. "He's alive."

A white boot emerged from the cloud of smoke. I gasped in disbelief at what I saw.

No... It wasn't possible, was it? How?

Before I stood Slate, holding the Orb of Death in his hand.

One of his white gloves had been badly burned. Slate's hand was blistered and blood soaked the glove.

Oh no.

He had caught the Orb of Death. But how was it possible?

Slate hurled it at me.

His spiders cheered and resumed fighting.

The Orb of Death quickly continued its chase, refusing to give up as I swirled, bombed, and flew in various loops.

I flew up in the air and headed for the ocean, diving into the water.

The Orb of Death stopped and hovered above the water.

I broke through the surface of the water and desperately fired a water bubble.

It hit the target.

There was a sound like crackling fire, and the Orb shrunk.

Bingo.

Solution? Water!

I hurled water bubbles at the Orb, though the ball dodged with ease and continued to pursue me, herding me away from the ocean.

"Oh!" I bumped into a solid figure and whisked around.

Faith, Olivia, and Lily cried, "Oh!"

"We're cornered!" Faith wailed, looking around. Three orbs hurled towards them, catapulted by Slate.

"What are those dark magic things?"

"Orbs of Death! Use Water bubbles!" I told them.

Faith, Olivia, and Lily nodded, and we formed a protective circle and shot water bubbles from outstretched palms.

"They're too fast! I can't get a single hit!" Lily cried in dismay, sweat beads forming on her forehead.

"Oh, no! Fluttering Fairies... The orbs are getting closer!" she warned.

"We're done for..." Olivia whined, bracing herself for the impact.

The Orbs of Death pelted closer and closer...

I squeezed Faith's hand. Faith shut her eyes tight and huddled closer.

"Pia!" Faith wailed. "It was an honor to fight with you."

"Meet your Doom, fairies! Once the Orbs of Death reach you, you will die!"

Slate cackled, chomping noisily on black popcorn.

"You were entertaining, no doubt! But…"

Slate turned his yellow gaze on me.

"…too late, the show's coming to an end. And so have your lives!"

Chapter 21
THE LAST ATTEMPT

Saltwater showered over me.

CRACKLE!

Was I alive?

"Hey, Pia! You okay?" I opened my eyes and looked down.

In the water was Marissa, my mermaid friend with her sister Emily!

I pinched myself.

"I'm fine. What happened?" I blinked, and checked on my friends desperately, nudging them in the side.

Marissa sighed with relief, Emily bobbing up and down in the water excitedly.

"And it looked like we arrived just in time to save you," Marissa said.

"And I even held a big, big, BIG water bubble and threw it!" Emily pipped up. "At the black balls."

A mermaid's water bubble was gigantic, and I wasn't surprised that the Orbs of Death was no match for it.

"Great, Emily!" I smiled, and Emily grinned from ear to ear.

"We're here to help save Maui! And we're here with the help of our sea creature friends!"

Marissa swam to the side and behind her, were sea turtles, dolphins, whales, sharks, orcas, sea horses, and many more creatures!

"Thank you! Thank you! For everything!" Faith exclaimed, hugging Marissa before I had the chance to even open my mouth. "Without you, we would have been goners!"

"You're the best!" I hugged Marissa too, as Olivia and Lily thanked Marissa gratefully.

"We're fighting with you, and yes that means Emily too. Against Slate of Chaos and his army of giant spiders." Marissa nodded, determination shining in her emerald green eyes.

"Nice." I gave her a quick summary of everything that had happened after entering the cave. "You're not just saving Maui, but the world and Friendship too."

Suddenly I thought of something.

When I had lured the Orbs of Death towards Slate, he had caught them using his bare hands, er, he was wearing his white gloves.

His gloves had withstood the powerful burn of the Orb of Death!

"Shall we?" Faith and Marissa chimed, snapping me back to reality.

There was a twinkle in Faith's hazel eyes. Marissa's emerald green eyes glinted. They looked at each other in surprise.

"We shall. ATTACK!" I let out a battle cry as Slate looked at us, annoyed by our joyful spirit.

"Let's save Friendship!" My friends nodded and cheered in agreement.

The sea creatures let out shrieks, chitters, and whoops.

"Save Slate for me!" I patted Emily's shoulders in comfort before taking off.

"For Friendship!" I screamed and dove down feet first.

Marissa and Emily swam as close as they could to the Friendship Point.

We were met by streaks of violet lightning, like the one that had killed Eel.

Marissa directed streams of water at the spiders.

I neared Slate, a few wingspans away.

Slate quickly thrust his hands forward as I paraded forward.

A purple beam of light – a death beam - blasted from his palms and incinerated a strand of my loose hair.

Slate took another aim.

I sped forward and landed in front of him and grabbed his arm, refraining him from using his magic.

I took the chance to aim a water bubble, but Slate broke free from my grip.

Slate leaned back and the water bubble whizzed over his head, missing him completely.

I prepared for hand-to-hand combat, sending a few rapid punches at Slate.

"The nerve of you! To come back!" Slate sneered at me, ducking my fist.

I panted, shooting another water bubble as I neared, less than a wing length away.

I kicked him, but Slate blinked and stuck out his tongue as if I hadn't touched him.

"Hey, what does Pinena mean, anyway?" Slate jeered. "Miserable little pine cone?"

"Excuse me, but Pinena means traveler!"

"In what, crybaby language?" He stuck his tongue out again in mock disgust and caught my leg.

I struggled to get free and batted my wings in his face.

Suddenly an arc of water sprouted from the ocean and battered Slate, and he let go of my wrist.

"Thanks, Marissa!" I yelled, and Marissa nodded in the distance.

Slate sent a death beam at Marissa, but luckily, she dived underwater in the nick of time, the beam missing her by inches.

"Don't pick on my friends!" I yowled, feeling a surge of anger and protectiveness, and flew behind Slate, kicked him on the back, and attempted to pin him to the ground.

But the evilest villain in the word wasn't finished.

"Don't expect me to lose to one fairy and a cowardly mermaid?" Slate whirled around and twisted my wrist with one hand.

"Yes." I let out a scream of shock and anger as he pulled my wings with his other hands.

Slate held one hand above me.

I gasped, moving my neck out of the way.

I froze as his hand closed on my throat.

"Puny." Slate cooed and tightened his grip. "Take your time to die. Suffer, fairy! No one can help you now!"

I kicked his chest and he stumbled back looking surprised, though his grip on my neck stood firm.

Apparently, he didn't expect a "Puny little fairy" to fight back.

But I was limp with exhaustion, and I could feel my face slowly turning purple.

How long could I keep this up?

Slate lifted me into the air and swung me around as if I was merely a doll he could play with.

My fingers tried to unclench Slate's grip. No success.

I reached for my pocket knife, stabbing it into Slate's glove. It ripped fabric and tore through flesh. Blood trickled down the cut.

But before I could do anything else, Slate quickly grabbed my pocket knife and flung it into a palm tree.

I felt my eyes roll up and meet Slate's gaze, not afraid to puke in his evil face.

"Are you dead yet?" he grumbled, a wicked grin spread across his face. "DIE THEN!"

Slate shook me, and I sagged down and bit his arm. It smelt like blood and tasted like death.

I couldn't take it much longer as Slate whirled me in the air like prey.

And right now, I WAS prey.

My every movement became feebler than the last, and I could barely feel the pain in my forehead from the Death Ball.

NO! STAMINA! GRIT! Oh, is it too late?

I felt my world become blurry….

I tried to move Slate's hand off my neck, and bit down onto his arm again.

I grew dizzy with each attempt and hoped it would be over quickly.

Distinct voices roared.

Someone screeched.

"You will not touch our heroes, Slate of Chaos!"

I felt Slate's grip slacken, then let go of me.

I dropped to the ground with a gasp and gulped in fresh air.

My back pounded on the pavement as I landed.

The sky whirled.

Small black dots danced in front of me.

Darkness shrouded my vision.

I passed out.

Chapter 22
THE FINAL BATTLE

Black.

I blearily opened my eyes.

"Hey! You okay there?" I blinked and saw a fairy standing over me, holding a spear in one hand and my pocket knife in the other.

Another fairy knelt over me.

"If you count almost suffocating, yeah, I'm fine." I croaked sarcastically. "Oh, sorry, I was being a bit cranky..."

I groaned as I tried to move. I turned, feeling the rough trunk of a palm tree brush against my shoulders.

"Oh, don't fret. You've been out for a while." The fairy smiled at me. "You stood your ground against Slate of Chaos when none of the villagers could land a single blow on Slate!"

The fairy kneeling over me glowed with green light and stepped back.

I touched my forehead, feeling my head wound. It was a scar now. "Wow!"

"I know some basic healing magic." The healing fairy said nervously.

"Thanks! I feel better already." I smiled back.

I tried to sit up, feeling my wings ache.

The healing fairy nodded at us and flew off to help more of the injured.

I craned my bruised neck to see several other fairies and fairy men fighting Slate of Chaos without too much luck.

My legs screamed as I feebly crawled forward.

"Here you go! You should be more careful!" The fairy instructed, handing me my pocket knife.

I noticed that half of her wing was severed.

"Thanks." I coughed and stretched my legs in a little warm-up. "What happened? There are so many people fighting Slate and his spiders!"

"We, the villagers, heard how you and your friends bravely fought Slate of Chaos and his spider army. You inspired us to fight too, not only for ourselves, but for Maui's future!"

The fairy wasn't finished talking yet.

"We will build trust in one another, and always will fight against evil. Leilani." Leilani held out a hand.

"Pia the Pinena Fairy." I shook her hand. "Nice to meet you!"

"You too. Alright. Back into the battle I go. Take care, you might want to rest your back before you start fighting again. Save Friendship!"

Leilani nodded at me and raced off into the jumble of life that was made up of creatures, villagers, and spiders.

Suddenly, a herd of horses burst out from nowhere and bucked into Slate's giant spiders. They chased the spiders towards the ocean where the sea creatures prowled in ambush.

I stumbled forward just as two villagers decided to attack Slate.

"Wait for me!" I rushed – or tried to – to the scene to help the two villagers but wasn't fast enough.

One villager raised his hands. His hands started glowing red, and little balls of fire emerged and swirled around Slate.

Slate swatted the fire, cursing, and the other villager lunged forward, whirling large rocks at Slate.

Slate's head whipped around and he caught the villager in the face with an accurate kick.

The villager stumbled backward in confusion, blood streaming from his nose.

Slate moved forward stealthily.

The villager controlling the fire quickly waved a hand, and the yellowed grass around Slate caught on fire.

Slate was trapped in the ring of fire, which continuedly grew and grew until it swallowed him from sight.

Then it started closing in.

The other villager retreated back to his comrade's side in a hopeful wait.

RUMBLE!

"That doesn't sound good," gasped the villager.

The vortex of fire dwindled and shrunk. The villager tried to take control of it, but the fire just got smaller.

There was a burst of smoke and flame, and Slate emerged, slender blue blades projected from both his gloves.

"Like my Huriblade? It'll make you hurry back to your mamas!"

He spun around, releasing the Huriblades. The two Huriblades twirled in the air like boomerangs.

They pinned the first villager to a palm tree and the second limply onto the ground.

Slate retracted his Huriblades like a panther retracted its claws.

I gritted my teeth. He was hurting so many people!

I took a flying leap forward and struck him on the chest.

Turning to look at me, Slate's lip curled in surprise. "The cowardly Pine fairy. Back for more, eh?"

"Again! It's Pia the Pinena Fairy!" I drew out my pocket knife, willing it to grow a little more to help me defeat Slate.

POOF!

There was a shimmer of magic, and my pocket knife grew bigger, until it was a sword! Rhinestones decked the sword's crossguard, and I could feel warmth emitting from them.

I gasped, numbly tracing my finger over the sword's blade.

"Oh yeah!" I grinned, feeling faint. I slapped my cheek to make sure I wasn't dreaming.

A dubious Slate was staring at my sword.

"But! How?" Slate stuttered, and suddenly a knowing look dawned in his eyes.

"Unless... It's the-the, sword?" he quickly caught himself and gained composure.

"It shape-shifts... it's final form... it all checks... No, I don't believe it! It's not true! It's just a legend..."

Slate shook his head, baffled.

"Anyway, no matter what weapon you carry, how weak or great, you're still no match for me! And Friendship will die! Join my side, Pia Pine fairy, and rule the world with me!"

"Over my dead body." I snarled, sword at hand. "And you didn't even pronounce my name correctly!"

Slate flung the Huriblades. "Too bad. I knew you would say that! Dead body it'll be!"

I retreated to the sky, the Huriblades tracing my movement. Slate followed in pursuit on a stormy thundercloud.

The Huriblades slashed at me, and I dodged nimbly. But one Huriblade swung at my pink skirt and hit my flesh.

"AGH!" I winced and slowed down.

I changed tactic and started shooting water bubbles at Slate's thundercloud.

The thundercloud boomed so loudly that everyone, even the spiders, turned to see all the commotion.

All eyes were on me and Slate now.

I hurled as many water bubbles as I could. Slate dodged a few and blocked most others, using unnecessary, captivating motions.

He made it look easy.

Show-off! I thought grimly, and dipped under him, fired upwards at the thundercloud, and zoomed to the side.

Slate's thundercloud jerked under the weight of the extra water and vanished.

Slate plummeted towards the ocean.

Everyone cheered, and the spiders groaned.

Suddenly, both Huriblades hurtled toward Slate. Slate flipped feet-first and landed on one Huriblade, using it as a replacement for the cloud.

He chuckled. "If you're going to fly, at least do it in style, Pine!"

Every fairy below me groaned, and the animals groaned in dismay too.

The spiders yowled in triumph. Commander Crusher gave a half-hearted cheer, chewing a wad of tree bark.

They continued fighting.

Slate glared at me. "Clever. I've got to hand it to you, tiny pine, that was clever."

"Gosh! How many times do I have to tell you? It's Pia the Pinena Fairy!" I declared a bit louder than I intended to.

"I say what I like, do what I like, and nothing will stop me!" Slate retracted a Huriblade and slashed at my face.

I ducked and flew underneath him.

"A formidable fighter." Slate chuckled darkly, dodging my sword. "The first real fighter in a few centuries."

"Centuries?"

Slate swung the Huriblade like a sword, and I struck out in defense just in time.

"Centuries?" I repeated. "What time do you live in? The potion and spell era? Wizard era? Don't tell me you're three hundred years old!"

"Beep! Wrong answer! Actually, I'm older!" Slate swerved forward and socked me in the guts.

"I don't age, you see!"

I froze momentarily in surprise. "But, then, how did you catch the Orb of Death with your gloves? They would have burned! Who has gloves strong as yours?"

I quickly dodged Slate's Huriblade as he zoomed forward.

"Dark magic keeps me alive, you see!" Slate snarled. "I have an extended lifespan. I can live to be a million years! Or older!"

"But you would die from a bad injury, wouldn't you?" I pondered. "You can be defeated!"

Slate dove at me again and I swerved to the side. His arm swept over me, and I leaned back.

As a result, I was whacked in the head, and his touch left dust on my forehead.

"EW! Dust!" I wiped it off.

I lunged, then at the last second swerved upwards over him and glimpsed the dust and lint on his sleeve.

I waved my sword, but it clanged with Slate's chest-piece.

"Your shirt is an awful choice of apparel!" I raised an eyebrow as Slate swiveled around.

"This is my favorite shirt! It has drops of blood from all my enemies since what, five centuries back?" Slate cackled, clashing his Huriblade with my sword.

"And I'll take your blood too!"

"Great. That's disgusting. And where did your sense of fashion go?" I mocked, trying to provoke him. "What a bore!"

"Curse you!" Hissing, Slate lunged forward and I side-stepped in the air.

Whirling around with astonishing speed, Slate slashed at my face.

I held up my sword in protection, but Slate's blade cut my elbow.

I yelped in pain.

"You've been a thorn in my side!" Slate hissed. "Or maybe a thin pine?"

I struck his arm with my sword in return.

The fabric ripped but Slate didn't notice or he just didn't care.

"Time to destroy you!"

He chased me high into the sky where the air was thinner.

I retaliated by swinging my sword menacingly every time he neared me.

Below, a giant hermit crab sloshed through the water, cramming spiders in its mouth.

Water sprayed into the air, acting like a barrier between Slate and me. I flew around it and caught Slate by surprise.

We sparred, and most of the time Slate would gain the upper hand.

Rarely would I get the chance to strike him.

Soon, I was gasping for breath.

"The air's thin. Extra movement, the more air you need." Slate noted, an evil thought forming in his wrenched mind. "You're weaker now! I'll eliminate you, and every other Friendship talent fairy in the world!"

He charged forward.

"I-I have the stamina… to defeat you!" I summoned up my remaining strength, and slid to the side. But not enough.

Slate collided into me, and I felt ice-cold hands close on my wings for a split second.

I fell.

My wings frantically fluttered, but didn't move and I couldn't fly up.

Twisting around, I saw dark magic restricting my wings.

I fell.

Then, POW!

I landed on something fuzzy and uneven.

Groaning, I clambered to my feet. A forest of green algae flourished below me on a big shell.

A pair of big eyes were staring curiously at me.

I looked down.

I was standing on the giant hermit crab!

"Sorry!" I apologized.

The hermit crab didn't hear me. "A fairy... Those legs look funny."

Commander Crusher took the opportunity and attacked, raking his pinchers across the hermit crab's chin.

The hermit crab turned away from me and pinned Crusher to a rock jutting from the water.

With a squeal of fear, Commander Crusher slipped free and dashed onto shore, and into the forest.

I blinked in surprise at his cowardice.

Turning around, I was cut off by Slate, who didn't at all seem to care that his lead and only commander was fleeing from the battle.

"How crabby are you going to get?" Slate snickered, and opened his mouth to say something snarky.

I head-butted him in the chest sharply and rebounded, rubbing my head.

He hacked up blood and glared at me. "I'll *cough*, get you!"

Suddenly, Faith, Olivia, and Lily flew up from behind him each holding a section of a black rope twined with a silver web.

Olivia whirled the rope like a cowgirl, flung it, and wrapped Slate up tightly.

"What?" Outraged, Slate spun around, having recovered from my headbut.

"How dare you! Ropes will not hold the powerful Slate of Chaos!"

Faith winked at me. "Slate can't use his magic when his hands are bound so tightly!"

"Good thinking." I smiled.

Slate growled in protest as we carried him off to the Friendship stands.

A giant frog ribbited and sat on a spider in our path as we neared.

The remaining spiders fled into the forest, seeing their leader tied up. Slate grunted his disapproval.

"Can you spare anyone to guard Slate for us while we deal with the Friendship stones?" Lily asked a group of villagers.

They were helping the wounded and a few others villagers were looking around, making sure the spiders wouldn't come back.

Leilani stepped out from the small group and nodded towards me, her knee banged up.

"Come, Kalei, Iolana, Kai." Two fairies and a fairy man stepped out from the group and followed us.

Their eyes darted to Slate of Chaos. He hissed at them, and Iolana drew back shivering.

The wind tickled my nose and I looked back.

Leilani's hands moved in such a fluid motion, I could barely see them as they whizzed in the air.

A vortex of wind was created, trapping Slate in it. An ideal prison.

Suddenly, a spider staggered out from behind a bush, reaching for Slate.

Leilani whipped around and thrust her hand forward before any other fairy could move.

A powerful blast of wind repelled the spider and shot it into a tree.

"Hurry! Watch the Friendship fairies do their thing!" Leilani exclaimed. "I can't wait!"

"How does it work?" I asked. "Remind me."

"It's a difficult but astounding process." Olivia looked at me.

"The Friendship energy will be released from the three Friendship stones. Then it shoots towards the Rainbow stone in the middle of the triangle."

Olivia pointed at the Rainbow stone.

"That will light up the Rainbow stone, which aggregates the Friendship energy to light up the Friendship Fire crystal, which is on top of it. You can FEEL the energy! It will be so cool!"

Faith, Olivia, and Lily hurried to their Friendship stands and took out their Friendship stones.

"In the name of Friendship, we will restore the peace and Friendship of the world." Faith whispered solemnly.

I turned, blinded, as a bright light shone from Faith's stone, then Olivia, and Lily's.

The lights were about to hit the Rainbow stone in the middle of the triangle.

Suddenly, a black orb appeared around the Rainbow stone. The black orb soaked in the Friendship energy like a sponge.

"You'll never save Friendship!" Slate cackled. "I took extra precautions to stop you! When the Friendship energy goes towards the Rainbow stone, my magic orb will appear and stop the Friendship energy!"

"It's time for darkness to rule once again!" he laughed madly.

I looked up to where his legs pointed like an arrow, and gasped.

The sun was setting!

Faith noticed this at once.

"OH NO!" she wailed. "Hurry, Pia, break that orb thing around the middle stone, The Rainbow stone. Once we start releasing the Friendship energy, we cannot stop until it is done!"

"We have to finish this ritual before the sun sets..."

Faith gulped. "...or Friendship is gone forever!"

Chapter 23
SAVING FRIENDSHIP

I headed for the black orb.

Raising my sword, I whacked the orb with all the energy I could muster. My sword slashed through it like it was air.

"What?" I couldn't believe my eyes.

I experimentally tapped the orb with one finger. But it was solid at my touch.

Why did my sword go through it?

My finger burned, and I looked at it.

The very touch of the orb had burned through my fingertip like acid.

"OW!" I quickly withdrew my hand. Blood welled up on a cut on my finger.

I touched the orb with the tip of my sword and my hand at the same time to see what would happen.

A wave of darkness swept over me and I staggered back, momentarily blinded.

"ACK!" I winced.

"It's been spelled!" Faith anxiously eyed the orb. "Don't give up, Pia! You've got to try to break that orb!"

"We're doomed!" I heard someone wail. "Fluttering Fairies..."

"No, we're not!" Leilani snapped at them. "I'm not one to give up, and neither are the Friendship fairies!"

Friendship must reign over the darkness.

Friendship will break the orb, darkness never shall have its victory. Friendship, help me defeat Slate and his magical powers, Friendship, find the weak point of this orb!

Oh please, oh please!

"Oh no you don't!" Slate growled.

With a mighty roar, he destroyed the wind vortex and the ropes binding him.

The wind vortex turned purple and hovered around Leilani, then evaporated.

Leilani collapsed, her skin pale. Iolana stood in front of her, shielding Leilani bravely from Slate.

Clomp.

Stomp.

Clatter.

The villagers charged forward holding weapons, and Slate waved a hand.

Dark magic surrounded the villagers and encased them.

"You won't defeat me!" Slate breathed, and with him he seemed to bring darkness that urged the sun to sleep forever.

He shambled forward.

"Pia! Hurry!" Faith screamed as Slate reached out a cold hand that clasped around her wrist.

Kai and Kalei rushed forward to pull Slate back, but Slate wouldn't budge.

Faith stood there, petrified in fear. "Pia!" her wails echoed in my ears.

"I can't break the black orb!" I crossed my fingers.

"But I have a hunch... and a plan..."

"Than what are you going to do?" Faith shrieked. "Pia!"

"Trust me." I hovered above the Rainbow stone.

The Friendship energy from the Friendship stones struck my body.

I was filled with warmth and energy.

Care...

Compassion...

Peacefulness...

Friendship...

My skin was tingling like crazy, glowing and shimmering.

I was one with Friendship.

My precious memories with my friends came back to me.

I remembered helping Emily create her first water bubble, Buttercup's cheeriness, saving Faith, Lydia showing us the way, finding Faith's friendship stone...

The eel sacrificing herself for Friendship...

And being saved from Slate by the villagers...

I let out a gasp.

The Friendship energy from within me shot up towards the Friendship Fire crystal above me.

The ginormous Friendship Fire crystal glowed a shade of rosy red.

The crystal began thumping, like a beating heart.

"Hear that?" I whispered to Faith, awestruck.

"Hear what?"

"The beating! The beating of the heart! The heartbeat of Friendship!" I declared loudly.

"No." Faith blinked at me, showing a set of pearly white teeth. "I can't hear much over Slate's wailing."

Slate's screams could be heard as the crystal gave a loud shower of sparkles.

Light flooded the whole of Maui and spread to the rest of the world.

It was just in time. The sun sunk below the horizon.

The Friendship stones jolted up from their stands, then whisked into the air.

They shot in the sky in different directions.

In the blink of an eye, they were gone, waiting for the next ten years...

...when the hunt for the Friendship stones would begin all over again.

I looked down.

The black orb underneath me had evaporated in the warmth of Friendship.

Light escaped the orb to reveal the rock in the middle, the sparkling Rainbow stone.

Everyone had a grin plastered on their face in a look of awe and amazement.

"We did it!" I cheered, grinning. "We did it! We saved Friendship and the world from Slate!"

I did a cartwheel in the air and landed by Faith.

Slate shrieked in horror.

I turned around to face him.

Slate's shoulder slumped forward, turning into dust.

His legs collapsed, his body decomposing. His skin peeled back and the bone underneath disintegrated.

"I'll get you back someday! I will! I will!" Slate screamed and lashed out at us.

"And Slate of Chaos is true to his word!"

"I'll come back, Pia the Pinena Fairy! You'll regret this! It won't be the last you'll see of me!"

His face crumpled, and his white glove fell onto the ground as he made one last effort to reach us.

And then he was gone, a pile of ash that blew away in the wind.

His white, torn, tattered, glove lay on the ground.

"Is Slate dead?"

Faith asked nervously.

"He was defeated. Slate of Chaos has been defeated!" I proclaimed.

This day would go down into history!

"We did it! We saved Friendship!" I cheered with Faith, Olivia, and Lily.

I fingered my sword. It shrunk back into a pocket knife, and I slipped it in my knife case.

My face hurt, my back hurt, my legs hurt, and my bones were aching.

My palms were bleeding, my hair was slightly frizzled and bruises lined my legs. Cuts and slashes bordered my arm.

I felt victorious with my friends.

Happy and satisfied.

Calm.

"So, basically to save the world..." Leilani limped forward, her face flushed with excitement.

"... well, you stood in as a replacement for the Rainbow stone!"

I smiled. Leilani wasn't finished.

"AND you were struck by Friendship energy!" Leilani yelled, her eyes scanning over me. "How COOL is that! Plus, I could swear your wings are sparkling!"

I turned, happy to confirm my wings WERE sparkling.

Was awesomely rad wings part of being struck with Friendship? What a great superpower!

The ocean waves could be seen peacefully beating against the shore from where I stood.

Splash!

The giant hermit crab sloshed through the water, onto the sand.

Then it shrunk and picked up a new shell. Joining its friends, it disappeared into the ocean.

"Never underestimate the Nui hermit crabs, who have the power to turn into giants!" Leilani remarked. "The biggest surprises can be found in the smallest form. And watch out for the magnificent ka lio seahorses!"

I smiled to myself.

As she spoke, the horses galloped up to their chests in the water. They turned into chest-nut brown, pearly white, and black seahorses.

Dolphins chirped in success. A pod of orcas chittered to each other happily and dived in the ocean.

The villagers walked forward, no longer frozen by Slate's magic.

"Thank you. We can never thank you enough for what you have done today." One villager said, his deep voice ringing with authority. "Friendship fairies, thank you. Pia the Pinena Fairy, thank you."

Faith, Olivia, and Lily all looked redder than tomatoes.

"Oh, yes! And this is Slate of Chaos' glove." I scooped up the glove and handed it to him.

The villagers bowed to us.

We bowed back.

My friends looked like they were about to explode.

I grinned, blushing profusely.

The joy of saving Friendship and defeating Slate was fresh in my mind.

I sat down on the ground, exhausted, and took out my shape-changing pocket knife and the magical map.

I had gotten these precious belongings from my dad.

But where did my dad get them from?

Leilani patted me on the shoulder and left.

I started in surprise. I was just in time to see Leilani fly away in a whirl of wind.

"Come on!" Faith exclaimed energetically pulling me to my feet. "Let's head for Maui town center for some the best extraordinary, exclusive, Maui shaved ice you'll ever taste!"

"Sounds good."

Faith, Olivia, and Lily flew up to leave and I followed, stopping to look back at the Friendship Point as we flew away.

The villagers cheered.

"It's been a great adventure." Faith reflected dreamily.

"Yeah." I smiled. "We learned one thing for sure. If we try our best with stamina and grit, anything is possible."

"What do you guys want to do after the shaved ice?" Lily mused thoughtfully.

"Yeah! I know! Let's have a luau to celebrate! Have you seen a luau yet, Pia?" Faith asked.

"Can't say I have."

Lily grinned. "It will be a great feast, and I'm sure you guys have worked up an appetite. We'll enjoy performances, and play games and hula. It will be the best luau ever!"

"Alright! Let's go!"

Friendship had been restored, and Slate had been defeated. All was well.

But now it's time to say bye, and I'll see you in my next daring adventure with me, Pia the Pinena fairy!

By the way, look down below to see the newest edition of the newspaper Flying Fairies!

Flying Fairies

Saving Friendship and Defeating Slate of Chaos!!!

Just as the world was about to give up Friendship, four astounding young fairies battled Slate of Chao and his giant spider army. The fairies were none other than the Friendship fairies named

Faith, Olivia, Lily, and their good friend Pia the Pinena fairy.

The four fairies gave Slate all they had. Mermaid Marissa and her sister Emily rounded up sea creatures to help in the battle.

"Pia has always been a good friend to me from the moment we met," says Marissa. "She was clever and smart with many skills and wowed me many times."

It was also rumored that Lily's pixie, Buttercup, passed away in an attempt to fetch help when her friends were in trouble.

When questioned about this Marissa the mermaid replied, "Buttercup the pixie will be missed greatly for her spirit, her cheerfulness and kindness."

Pia, Faith, Olivia, and Lily were interviewed at the local Koleamoku Hut.

They wore many cuts and slashes across their skin but were proud of their accomplishment.

Fans came flying in a minute later and soon they were pampered with questions.

"Why can't I see friendship?" asked a fan. "Is it invisible?"

"You're right. You can't see Friendship, nor hear it. But you CAN feel it, right here in your heart." Pia told the eager audience.

"It's inside of everyone. You just need to find it." Pia smiled.

"In this adventure, what I learned most is about stamina and grit. If you keep trying your best with stamina and grit, anything is possible!"

Immerse yourself in the wonderful world of

Pia the Pinena Fairy!

Pia the Pinena Fairy

The Moondust Adventures

Come and join me in this daring quest!
In the searching for my fairy talent, I rescued my
mermaid friends Marissa & Emily from the spells of evil
elves. I unlocked the epic Moondust mine, reversing the
fate for the cursed Magicores. We evaded the crazy
monkey king, and fought the vicious flock of viral
vultures. Plus, I encouraged my bird friend Harmonica
to build friendship with her old archenemy and they
worked together to win The Best Bird of the Year
contest. And the best part? During this great adventure,
I found the true and MAGICAL meaning of Friendship!

Pia the Pinena Fairy
The Moondust Adventures

Combo
2 stories in 1

By Amy Zhao

Pia the Pinena Fairy

The Legendary Judges of Magic

In this action-packed adventure, I journeyed with my Magicore friend Furball and our fairy friend Sapphire. We had close encounters with amazing creatures and scary monsters, and nearly drowned in the churning river of many whirlpools. We even battled against a huge, deadly fire-breathing dragon! We did all this in a race to pass the tests from the Legendary Judges of Magic. The results? We discovered something truly astonishing and rewarding.

Pia the Pinena Fairy

The Legendary
Judges of Magic

By Amy Zhao

110 pages full of adventures and fun!

New!

Including writing tips and lessons I found that may help everyone write their own stories!

Pia the Pinena Fairy

Saving Maui

Now you have experienced all the adventures with Pia in this story!

Do you think you can write a review for this wonderful story? Share it with your friends, or work with your parents to share it online. When you post a review, I will be able to see it.

Thank you!
- Amy Zhao

This book

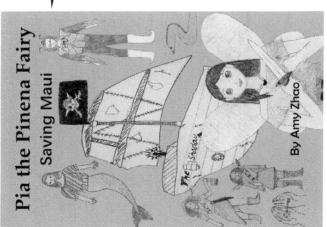

Pia the Pinena Fairy
Saving Maui

By Amy Zhao

52228691R00191

Made in the USA
Middletown, DE
09 July 2019